The Orchardist's Secret

Ray Mathews

BLACK ROSE
writing™

ISBN: 978-1-61296-475-1

PUBLISHED BY BLACK ROSE WRITING

www.blackrosewriting.com

Printed in the United States of America

Suggested retail price $15.95

The Orchardist's Secret is printed in Adobe Garamond Pro

To my long-time editor, Sally Mathews,
who has made my books shine with her knowledge and patience.

The Orchardist's Secret

To my neighbors and friends,
Lisa and Tom Dunham

Ray Mathews

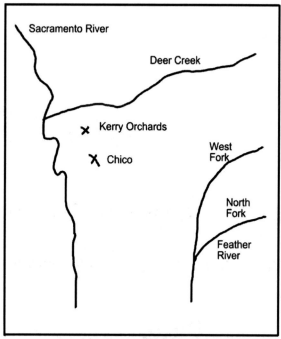

Northern California

PROLOGUE

Sean Kerry loved his orchards; he devoted his life to growing the best fruits, for to him his fruits were like gold – until the Yamadi Maidu Indians promised him the real thing.

In early 1847, after they came to work in Sean's orchards, and grew to love the 'Fruit Chief', the Indian boys wondered why he wanted the gold nuggets. In the Maidu culture, the 'yellow stones' made good jewelry for their mothers, or a token hung around the neck on a leather thong, but to Sean Kerry the nuggets meant a fortune in the white man's world.

What if the Maidu *did* give me a few gold nuggets? Sean wondered. Could I spend them? And what could happen if I did?

Speculative questions, but questions that should be answered, so Sean searched the Chico, California library to find out what happened after a gold nugget appeared in other places, in other times. His research was difficult since the library was not large, but he persevered with the help of the old librarian, Mrs. Calm, who borrowed books from other places.

In every case from the 1500's to the 1800's from Mexico to the Carolinas, he found that the same results occurred: greed, thievery, loss of property, thousands of innocent people uprooted, bad water, ruined soil, game killed, crime, and mass murder—all because of a bright and yellow metal.

Sean tossed and turned for an hour; finally put his feet on the floor, rose, and glanced back at his sleeping wife, Jennifer. He left the room, walked to the porch, and sprawled on the step.

He looked over his orchards in the pitch black night with only the dim stars above, and knew, even though he couldn't see them, that his plants were healthy, the tree trunks sturdy and strong, the limbs pliant, the bark tight on the trunks, the leaves dark green, the fruits fragrant and ripening; he could feel the life of his fruit in his fingers, even though he didn't touch it, their skins like that of a young woman, soft, pliable, alive — his apples, apricots, plums, and pears.

Sean Kerry's treasure.

He knew he had a dilemma.

He could cause the disaster he'd read about if he displayed even *one gold nugget* to a white man. For no one had ever seen gold around here... until now.

That Sean might lose his beloved orchards deeply disturbed him.

He knew that he must hide the Maidu gold, never use it, as if saving for a rainy day which may never come.

He must warn the Maidu Indians to keep their gold secret from covetous white men.

Sean remembered the days seven months ago when he rode from Nevada to California in search of new orchards to replace his ruined ones, the days when his new life began ...

Chapter 1

March 1847

In late March of 1847 near the Truckee River, Sean Kerry woke to a morning of aches from sleeping under the stars on cold hard ground, not used to living in the rugged outdoors, for as a fruit-growing orchardist with several orchards to tend, the disaster of Fire Blight had decimated his Wadsworth, Nevada orchards and forced him to look elsewhere.

But this trip took him toward a new beginning in his life, or so Sean hoped.

When he rose, he found a light coat of snow on his blanket and ground cover and in the thinned-out leaves of the cottonwood trees around him; he shook out his blanket and went right to his chores, shaking off the chill of the remaining winter weather. His breath came out in white mists as he looked around his camp site. Water came first for him and his old horse, Martin, and then he cooked a meager breakfast of cornmeal cakes and sour coffee, nowhere close to the breakfasts his wife, Jennifer, made for him. He shaved and felt human again, cleaned up his campsite, and scattered the ashes from his fire.

As he rode away from his overnight camp, Sean raised his hat and spanked the light snow off the brim as he scanned the countryside around him. To his left were rocky cliffs with a few gnarled trees growing out of the rocks, and on his right on the other side of the Truckee River he spied a few rolling hills that might make a good orchard if a man wanted to try at this elevation. Plenty of water and drainage for fruit trees, he thought, but he had better prospects in mind and hopefully in a better climate.

After several hours on the trail along the Truckee River the terrain became hilly with lots of loose rock. With his old horse, Martin, about done in, Sean walked him through this rocky part of the Sierra Nevada most of the afternoon while he scanned the hills and cliffs in search of a trail or a sign of life, but only animal trails appeared. These loose rock trails had slowed Sean considerably, and he had already lost at least one day on his trip toward Chico, California. He didn't want to overtax his old horse.

The river had a thin coating of ice along the edge because of the low temperature last night, and he needed water. He took off his gloves, broke the thin ice, submerged his empty canteen, and let the cold water fill it. He rested near the water's edge where he noticed Valley Oak trees and wild grape vines in abundance, a sure sign that he had reached California.

As he sat resting, looking at the rocky base of the sheer cliffs overlooking the Truckee River, Sean thought of his family and his orchardist heritage.

* * *

Sean's father, Ryan Kerry, an orchardist in Wadsworth, Nevada, taught Sean all he knew over the years. Fruit trees became Sean's life time ambition, so naturally Sean taught his only son, Finn, all he knew and at times thought Finn had caught the orchard bug like Sean and his father, but Finn had other yearnings, too. He wanted to be a writer, and at twenty-three actively worked on his first novel while a junior editor for Hanford Publishing Company in Reno, Nevada, about thirty-five miles west of the present Kerry orchards. He chuckled as he thought of how Finn resembled him; medium height with light-brown hair, thin, and as his wife Jennifer described him, lanky. People had mistaken Finn for Sean's brother more than once.

If blame became necessary on Finn's change in attitude toward fruit-growing, Sean blamed Finn's mentor Gerald Mann. A literary scholar and senior editor with Hanford, Mann guided Finn from the beginning of his career with publishing, and finally convinced Finn to take the leap from short stories to writing his first full-length novel.

Now Finn thought of nothing else, and even though Finn disappointed Sean by not being enraptured by fruit trees, Sean understood that Finn had a drive about writing just as Sean had about growing fruit. For some reason, Finn would not tell Sean the title of his new book.

Stymied in his efforts to entice Finn into the Kerry family orchard business, he watched as Finn made his way in the world of the written word, hoping that one day he would come back to the fold and take over the orchards when Sean retired in the future.

At forty-six when disaster struck the Kerry orchards in Wadsworth, Sean knew in his heart that with the loss of the family orchards he would probably never see Finn become a plant lover like Sean and his grandfather.

* * *

He rode south from Wadsworth, Nevada, his home, and followed the Truckee River to the west whenever possible, sometimes with open fields to the north and south of the river and at other times, low mountain ranges with rugged cliffs rising steeply on both sides of the Truckee. Most of the trees near the river he recognized as Aspen and Cottonwood, but once in a while he noticed pine and fir trees off toward the mountains, many still sprinkled with light snow.

In his correspondence with orchardist, Miles Bracken, whose orchards lay almost due north of Chico, California, beyond the foothills of the Sierra Nevada Mountains, Bracken had discussed the severity of the previous winter experienced by the Donner party. He explained to Sean that his orchards lay well past the foothills of the Sierra Nevada, in fact, almost to the Sacramento River, and seldom experienced the snows of the mountain range although winters could be cold.

Bracken mentioned that John Fremont and Kit Carson came down the Truckee River in 1844 and initially named it the Salmon Trout River; however, later, they renamed it after their Indian guide, Chief Truckee, who earlier guided an immigrant party from the headwaters of the Humboldt River and the Carson River to California.

He also mentioned Alta California in which the Bracken orchards grew, a huge territory which neither Spain nor Mexico had ever colonized. No effective government control had ever extended much beyond southern Arizona and coastal California. Native American Indians remained in possession of most interior regions of Alta California.

The Mexican-American War was all but over, Alta California sat on the brink of becoming a territory of the United States. They talked about a treaty to be signed at Villa de Guadalupe Hidalgo. Once that happened, Sean felt certain that California might soon become a state, and the Indians would quickly lose their lands. It had happened in other parts of the United States, and it would happen in California, too, he thought.

From the map Sean had acquired, the Truckee River ran from a lake called Tahoe in California where many Washoe Indians lived and fished during the summers, to the east and then north in Nevada to Pyramid Lake north of Sean's old orchards, and as a guess, the Truckee River spanned about 70 miles.

He knew from Bracken's directions that he had to leave the Truckee River when it turned south toward Lake Tahoe, and he must continue west till he picked up the Yuba River and then continue west to Yuba City. Then he would turn north to Chico and once at Chico he could get directions to the Bracken Orchards from Jon Simms at the general store.

Sean knew that Deer Creek, a tributary of the Sacramento River, ran east from the Sacramento River about 71 miles, but flowed west, winding through steep canyons filled with rapids, and also containing beautiful green fields sloping perfectly for orchards and gravity irrigation.

* * *

Sean felt Martin give a loud snort and dismounted, for he knew the horse might collapse. He poured a little water into his hand and let Martin slurp it. The highest part of the Sierra Nevada Mountains was behind him, and he kept heading east as the temperature reached twenty-five degrees. The winds picked up and he put his kerchief over his nose and squinted.

He had to find shelter for the night and lose another day while his horse rested. He had taken a chance riding Martin on this trip; the horse had aged badly. He pulled his small oat bag from the saddle and fed Martin two handfuls. The horse's tongue lapped up the oats quickly and looked for more, but Sean had to conserve what he had for Martin till he could find some naturally-growing grass for him. Tomorrow they would descend into a warmer climate and find open fields, too.

Sean walked slowly, leading Martin carefully over the rocky terrain, looking for a sheltered place to spend the night when he saw the dark shadow of a recess in the rocks. He approached it slowly, and squinted against the dark opening in the cliff face. This looked like the place he wanted; good shelter from the piercing wind and a place to have a small fire. He pulled Martin under the overhanging cliff, hobbled him, and turned toward the small cave. You never know what might be harbored in a cave, he thought, and drew his knife from the scabbard on his belt just in case. Maybe he should have brought his Allen Pepperbox pistol after all. At least he would have three shots for protection. Of course, I feel over-cautious, he thought with a snicker; Jenn always says I am.

He moved into the cavern, his shoulder against the wall as he slid his feet carefully over the loose gravel. He moved six feet into the blackness in front of him when he heard something shift ahead, and a low, throaty growl came from close by in the cave.

Sean backed away, his knife held out in front of him, not sure which way to move.

He heard a plaintive whine and another attempt at a growl. An animal appeared to be hurt, thought Sean. He had to find out for sure before he could use the cave.

He returned to Martin, fished in the saddle bag for flint and steel and a blanket from behind his saddle, gathered an armful of small twigs and branches lying nearby, and re-entered the cave. By the wall near the entrance, he stacked his load of wood, and using the finest parts of the twigs and shaving more with his knife in the virtual darkness, struck the steel with the flint.

Another shift on the gravel came from across the cave and a short whine as the tinder flamed, and Sean nursed the flames into a fire. Once he could see, he scanned the cave, looking for whatever had growled. He thought he saw a grey shape across the cave against the far wall. He kept the knife ready, held the blanket in front of him, and continued to build up the fire. Now flickering shadows disappeared and he saw a shape that looked like a large dark grey wolf.

He took two steps toward the shape, and stopped when the mewling whine came again. Out of the darkness the animal bounded and tried to limp toward the entrance, and Sean could see that a steel trap had caught his front leg at the joint above the foot. He began to talk to the animal in soft tones while he edged closer and closer to the gaunt wolf, holding his blanket out in front like a shield.

Suddenly the wolf lunged, howled pitifully, and collapsed on the ground.

Silence covered the cave except for the crackle of burning wood. Outside he hardly heard the blustery wind. Sean looked across the three feet to where the wolf lay, quiet now, not moving, with his teeth scraping on the trap's razor-sharp teeth. The animal had evidently passed out from the pain, and Sean's sense of duty forced him to put away his fears and approach the wolf.

The starving beast lay unmoving, and in the firelight, Sean could see the wicked jaws of the trap and the dried blood along his leg. He must have been caught in the trap for days or longer, thought Sean. What can I do? He wondered. He had to open the trap somehow. He looked around and found a piece of limb about four feet long, approached the wolf, and touched the trap. The wolf gave no response.

In seconds, Sean wedged the limb into the trap, pulled one set of teeth away from the other, and slid the jaws away from the wounded foot. In another moment the wolf's foot slipped free. The foot looked badly damaged near the first joint. Bleeding had started again now that he had slipped the foot from the trap.

As he dropped the trap against the wall, the wolf awoke, raised his head, looked up at Sean, and dashed from the cave, limping badly as he passed Sean in his eagerness to flee. Sean called out to him as he fled, but his words were lost in the swirling harsh wind.

The wolf disappeared.

Sean lighted one end of the limb and held it like a torch while he explored the cave. From front to back the cave measured about twelve feet long and ten feet wide with more than enough height for him to stand erect.

He fed the fire, led Martin into the cave, removed the saddle and saddle bag, glanced around outside the cave for signs of the wolf, and finally settled near the fire for the night.

An hour later, he heard Martin whiney; his hoofs stirred the loose gravel in the cave as he moved about. Sean rose when at the center of the entrance to the cave he saw the grey wolf staring at him in the firelight. Sean grabbed his knife and prepared himself, but the wolf crept into the cave near the wall opposite Sean and collapsed on the cave floor with a long, whispered sigh. Sean watched the wolf; the thin grey animal's dancing yellow eyes flickered in the firelight and watched Sean as the weary wolf curled tightly against the wall. Sean didn't notice his own fatigue, but sometime later he must have relaxed and fallen asleep.

When Sean awoke in the morning the wolf had gone.

He packed his gear, fed and watered Martin, and set off for his destination. Later in the day as he led Martin down a hill into a protected valley, he glanced back at the hill top and saw the grey wolf standing in silhouette watching him. When Sean reached a small stream in the valley, he looked for the wolf again, but the wolf was gone.

* * *

The sun beamed down on him as he rode on, and before him laid a panorama of valleys and forests of dark green trees, still patched with light snow. He saw several deer and an elk. Earlier in the day two Indian boys passed him on an old pony with no saddle or harness, but simply a rope to guide him. He figured they were Paiute Indians and assumed they were friendly. The Paiute Indians had always been friendly near his home in Wadsworth, Nevada. Sean didn't carry a gun, but left his old three-shot Allen pistol and muzzle-loading Kentucky rifle with his wife, Jennifer, and his son, Finn, for protection, although when he left, he doubted they would need any weapons in the quiet orchard country of Wadsworth, Nevada.

When he bought the old Kentucky Flintlock muzzle-loader which had been converted in Texas to a percussion cap with a thirty-eight-inch barrel, the old prospector who sold it to him said that because of the percussion cap exploding the powder charge, the gun could hit a moving target since the response between trigger pull and powder explosion happened faster. This meant little to Sean as he saw a bargain in the guns and thought for the price he had found good home protection for his family. He hoped his wife, Jennifer, and son, Finn, could cope with loading the old guns the way he showed them.

Since orchardist Miles Bracken's warning about rampaging Paiute Indians, Sean felt concerned for his family because Bracken said the Paiute Indians had shot cattle and horses while the Donner settlers were attempting to pass through the Sierra Nevada range. Of course, this could have been because of the severe winter they were caught in when folks became frantic for food. Bracken had mentioned the possibility of cannibalism with the Donner party, so they must have been in desperate straits.

Sean pulled Martin to a halt, raised his hand to his hat brim, squinted and scanned ahead of him, hoping to see a noticeable trail or a sign of life in the fields to the west, and finally spotted a thin curl of smoke in the distance. He rode slowly into a camp where four hunters sat around the fire in blankets, fried a slab of bacon and cornmeal cakes, and eyed him with curiosity. He noticed the skins staked out and frozen meat hung from a tree limb. He asked for directions to Chico, California and they told him to keep going west till he saw the Yuba River and just follow that to Yuba City, then north to Chico. After sharing their breakfast, Sean prepared to leave.

'Ye'r not one a them gold prospectors are ye?' asked the leader of the hunters.

Sean laughed.

'Far from it. I'm a fruit-grower on my way to look at some new orchards east of Chico.'

'Okay. Seems like I see a lot of prospectors, but never heerd of no gold.'

The man sized him up again as Sean mounted Martin, and as he turned away from the camp, the man swatted Martin to get him started out of the camp.

'Hope that old nag makes it.'

Sean headed west on the road they mentioned toward the Yuba River, Yuba City, and Chico near where the new orchards lay, leaving the

Truckee River behind him as that river turned south at the men's campsite toward Lake Tahoe.

Chico lay about fifteen miles west of the Feather River which had two tributaries originating in the Diamond Mountains: the North Fork and the Middle Fork, both of which flowed east. The Nisenan Maidu Indians had lived on the North Fork of the Feather where they hunted and gathered for subsistence, but according to Bracken, ten years ago the Yamadi Maidu left the Nisenan. The Yamadi Maidu Indians were nomadic, broke their ties with the Nisenan Maidu who lived high in the mountains, and settled in the foothills near Deer Creek north of Chico and the Bracken Orchards.

He knew from Bracken that John Bidwell had named Chico when he bought his ranch and other businesses in the settlement after his arrival on one of the first wagon trains to reach the area in 1843, four years ago, and over time the name Chico had stuck even though the city had not incorporated. The original inhabitants were the Mechoopda Maidu Indians who worked for Bidwell for the same salary as white men, and Bidwell treated them fairly. In fact, Bracken mentioned that Bidwell had called a troop of cavalry from the south to protect the Mechoopda Indians once when white men threatened to exterminate them. Bidwell took an active part in the affairs of Chico.

The Yamadi Maidu Indians now lived about seven miles from Bracken's orchards, but were a friendly tribe with whom Bracken exchanged fruits for their pottery and leather goods, and labor for his orchards.

Sean rode into Chico, California a day later than he had expected, but no time for his arrival had been set. He sized up the town as he rode down the main street; false store fronts in a row for about three blocks, some two-story buildings of wood, busy merchants displaying their wares in front of stores set on a wooden walk with hitching posts along the street on both sides; a typical non-descript California town. He found Simms' General store, introduced himself to Jon Simms, asked for directions to the Bracken Orchards, and rode on.

* * *

17

Sean's fifty-five acres in Nevada of mostly apple orchards inherited from his father had been totally ruined by Fire Blight, a bacterial disease of apples and pears and other fruits that killed the blossoms, shoots, limbs, and occasionally the entire tree. Sean's orchards were a total disaster except for a small grove of apricot trees, and hopefully this trip would find him at new orchards and a new country to provide a home and new life for his wife, Jennifer and his son, Finn.

Sean wanted to start over with better orchards and more acreage if possible. And from what he'd heard, California was a grower's paradise, and Miles Bracken's orchards might be his answer. He knew he had to find new orchards while he still had the funds to get a new start.

Two months ago a friend, who had been visiting the coast in California, brought Sean a small ad from the newspaper, *The Californian*, a thin one-page newspaper, about an orchard for sale near Chico, California. The new orchards were located northwest of Chico, below Deer Creek and east of the Sacramento River. The For Sale ad seemed like a gift from heaven to Sean, and he began a correspondence with the owner, Miles Bracken, who desperately needed to sell because he'd gotten too old to properly care for his trees and wanted to leave something to his children who were not interested in his orchards.

Sean Kerry could sympathize with this as he thought of his son, Finn, and his writing. Bracken wanted to move in with his children and give them their inheritance early. He had indicated to Sean that his health had faded over the last two years, and he couldn't climb into the trees like he used to.

Sean desperately wanted to buy the property for his family if the land appeared acceptable. He figured that with the sale of his own fifty-five acres to his neighbor, Brigham Meister, Sean could make a substantial down payment on the new property and pay off the balance in about eight years, God willing. Meister knew Sean's orchards were a loss, but he wanted to clear the land and plant corn and other crops to expand his farm.

Miles Bracken had agreed to the mortgage terms Sean offered for his orchards and home. Now Sean had to see the property first hand.

Chapter 2

March 1847

Once to the west of the Sierra Nevadas, Sean approached Deer Creek from Chico, and became excited by the beautiful terrain filled with dark healthy pine trees at the base of low hills, miles from the mountains, and with good sources of water from large creeks flowing into the Sacramento River. He scanned the gently rising green hills searching for the orchards based on the directions of store-owner Jon Simms.

Soon he noticed several columns of fruit trees and rode the lagging Martin to a large home on an overlook. Sean studied the orchards with interest, and finally turned to the house. Could these be the Bracken orchards? Sean wondered. He looked in disbelief at the large, sturdy-looking house which Miles Bracken had agreed to sell as part of the deal. The house alone could bring a quarter of the price Bracken had quoted: broad front porch, two-story with gables across the front and a third floor room with a balcony. Bracken had mentioned five bedrooms for Bracken had five grown children, three boys and two girls, all married.

As he rode through the rows of apple trees, he looked about him at the several orchards; apples grew in abundance, and he saw more apples in another large orchard, and near the house a group of plum trees. He dismounted, tied his horse to a small tree, and walked around the side of the house where he saw what must be the experimental orchard Miles had mentioned.

He spotted numerous grafts on the trees. Mr. Miles Bracken appeared to be an orchardist after my own heart, Sean thought as he walked

19

directly to the apple trees and began to study the fruit, its healthy color, the dark green of the leaves, and the strength of the trunks and bark. At both sides at the base of each tree from row to row were clay pipes used for irrigation, with a drip system at work wetting the area close to the trees.

I am in heaven, thought Sean, unable to contain his excitement.

'You must be Sean Kerry,' said a weak voice from behind him. Sean turned, smiled, and shook the frail hand of tall Miles Bracken. The man appeared to be easily in his eighties; thin as a bamboo shoot, but with a fine head of white hair and a short beard; however, from his grip, he didn't seem too strong, and his hands shook as they exchanged greetings.

'Wal, what do you think, Mr. Kerry? Do you like the orchards?'

Sean turned around and round several times and exhaled with a beaming face.

'If all of the orchards look like this one, I like them fine, Mr. Bracken. Of course, I noticed some repairs are in order on some of the trees, but I can understand that you are not up to the work with a place of this size. Don't you have any help?'

Bracken chuckled. 'Had some. Had two local fellas for a year or two, but one up and left for Yerba Buena, and the other one started his own place nearer the Sacramento River. Not a lot of folks living near us here, and besides, they have their own crops to tend. Been using Maidu Indian boys lately. The Indian boys are always willing to work if I can find a few who will stand still to be trained. All they want is a few toys, metal tools for their fathers, sturdy cloth for their mothers and, of course, plenty of candy.' He laughed. 'The Maidu love candy.'

'Huh, never thought about using Indian labor before. So that works for you?'

'Oh yes, sure does. The Yamadi Maidu have a small village about seven miles north of here nearer the foothills close to Deer Creek. It's hard to get them interested in fruit trees, though they groom a forest of oak trees to get acorns for their winter food. You see, the Maidu are mainly hunters. They're nomadic, and I never know if they'll be here from one month to the next; they have a winter home and a summer home; they move with the game. Lucky for me, they summer here during my harvest seasons. They hunt with bows and arrows and sometimes use snares to catch small animals. The men are on the hunt most of the time, but the boys are often available if not off hunting with their fathers.

'A few of the men have old muzzle-loading rifles, but they're in the minority. They're pretty set in their ways, but they're friendly. They steer clear of white men as much as possible, since the whites haven't treated them well over the years. They've been friendly with me because I give them fruit out of every harvest. Their tribe consists of about sixty people. They split off years ago from the Nisenan Maidu who live high the Sierra Nevada's.

'Mr. Kerry, I was about to graft a new apple variety in my experimental orchard in back of the house. Want to come and take a gander?'

Sean nodded eagerly. 'Yes, and maybe I can do one myself. Your apples are as healthy as I've seen. And I noticed you have a drip irrigation system working. Where did you get the clay pipe? Must have been expensive...'

'Made all the pipe m'self, well, me and two of my boys. There's some clay soil up in the foothills and I just shave the clay into thin strips, wrap them on a wood mandrel, and let them air dry for a week. Then I remove the mandrel, punch drip-holes in the pipes, and kiln-fire the pipe in my shed over there, after I core the ends for a spigot connection. I use local cement or tar to seal pipe joints. Most times the tar works better than cement, and there's no mixing with the tar. 'Course, tar is ugly stuff to work with and hard to get off your hands and clothes.'

'Interesting. I'd sure like you to show me the pipe-making process. That's one of the best irrigation systems I've seen in operation.'

'Wal, I dammed a piece of the creek behind the house which stems from Deer Creek, made a good pond with a weir, and run water into the pipes from the pond when I want–usually once a day or less, depending on the rain fall and season. It's all gravity feed and doesn't take much tendin'. I usually open the weir at night and let it run till morning; nothing much to it.'

Sean glanced around the periphery of the orchards.

'Looks like your fences around the orchards needs some work...'

'Yes sir, the deer and other critters tear it up on occasion, and lately I don't have the energy to fix it, and all my help's about gone since I haven't been too active lately.

'Animals can be downright bothersome when the fruit starts to ripen, I can tell you, and there's lots of wildlife in the area if a man's interested in venison or skins. They like my young trees especially, so I have to watch them careful. From time to time prospectors wander through and I let them pick fruit if it's ripe enough, but they don't generally hurt my fences. Once in a while the Maidu hunters come by and take game nearby, so this helps save my fences somewhat.'

The old man watched Sean as he pruned the trees, spliced a new variety of fruit to a tree, wrapped the splice carefully, and handled the fruit with care, and Bracken knew he had found the right man to take over his orchards. Bracken showed him the apple, apricot, plum, and pear orchards, and Sean felt anxious to start work on these trees as soon as possible. He could already see what needed to be done. He couldn't wait to describe what he had seen to his wife and son.

Finally after viewing all the orchards, Sean toured the home with Bracken, who at every room explained his improvements. Sean had difficulty containing his joy with the house and returned to one room after another, especially the five large bedrooms. He noticed the beautiful glass windows, the large fireplace well-stocked with logs, the window placement for getting the best early morning breezes and shade in the afternoons, and the wide covered porch on the front well-shaded by several large oak trees.

'Early on when my wife was still around, I dug a well with the help of the Maidu Indians and put up a windmill to supply water to our kitchen. The hand pump in the kitchen still works just fine. Now I mostly just use the pumped water to keep the pond full.'

'My wife, Jennifer, would sure like that kitchen pump, I think.'

After Sean had seen the inside of the house, they looked at the other buildings on the property: the large shed in the rear used for a workshop, a kiln area, a fruit-storage building near the house, and a barn with stable and hay loft at one end. Finally, Sean told Bracken that he'd like to close the deal as he reached into his saddle bag and pulled out a cashier's check for a down payment. He made a cash down payment, wrote a note for the property, knowing Jennifer and Finn would adapt well to this beautiful home and orchards.

'You can wait to sign that check till we see my lawyer in the morning, Sean,' said Miles.

Sean stayed the night with Bracken, and early the next morning they rode into Chico in Bracken's wagon to see Bracken's lawyer, arriving just as the little city's commerce got underway. As Sean and Miles walked down the street toward the lawyer's office, two deputies passed them and tipped their hats. A few of the store owners were out sweeping the wooden sidewalks in front of their stores, and vendors were setting up shop along the street and looking for customers. Many said 'hello' to Miles Bracken, the local orchardist.

'Let's go to the lawyer's office, Sean, and let his secretary write up this contract. That'll take a while, so let's have some breakfast at Natty's while we're waiting. Tomlin never gets in before nine. We can see him arrive from inside. Lawyer Tomlin will be proud to use the new Morse Telegraph down the street. He can verify your check with your Wadsworth bank in minutes. Not like the old days when we had to send for a reply by the mails.'

Sean smelled the frying food and realized he felt hungrier than he thought and had three eggs, sausage, fried sliced potatoes, and coffee, while Bracken had nothing but coffee and toast with plum jelly, probably from his own orchard, Sean thought.

After a hardy breakfast, they entered Lawyer Tomlin's office, and surprisingly the contracts were already prepared. Sean and Miles read the contract, and Miles made one change and initialed it.

'All the furnishings go with the house,' said Bracken.

Tomlin shrugged and nodded. 'Okay, Miles. I need you both to initial that change.'

They signed the contract and had two witnesses from Tomlin's office sign also.

Bracken's lawyer had agreed to make the cash transfer from Sean's Wadsworth bank which would take several weeks to clear. He had already verified the check with Sean's bank.

Outside in front of the lawyer's office, Bracken turned to Sean.

'Wal, Mr. Kerry, you are now the owner of a wonderful orchard property. I hope it gives you as much pleasure as it has given me over the years.' Kerry looked away as he could see Miles getting choked up.

As the winter ended Sean could already feel temperatures moderating.

With Bracken's consent, he moved in immediately, and asked Bracken to stay with him for a month and teach Sean his growing methods. Meanwhile, Sean's wife and son made plans to join him as soon as they could.

He needed to repair many of the trees as the orchards had not been well tended for a year or more. He knew that his efforts to bring the orchards up to good yields would take about six months. He explained to Bracken about Finn's interest in writing, not sure if Finn would join them in the new property.

Bracken shook his head sadly. 'I reckon I can understand that, Sean. None a my boys are orchardists, either.

'You're gonna need some help pretty soon with the apricots and plums starting in May. Let me take you to the Maidu village and introduce you to Chief Sam. A word from him and you'll have all the help you need, as long as you agree to give them a few bushels of fruit from every harvest. All the Indian boys want in exchange for their work are a few toys, tools for their fathers, and cloth for their mothers – oh yes, and buttons. The Maidu women love buttons.'

Miles took Sean in his wagon, crossed Deer Creek at a low spot, and on to the Maidu village where Miles introduced Sean to the leader, Chief Sam, as the few white people who visited the village called him. Miles explained with signs and a few words that Sean would need help with his harvests soon, and would like to use the Indian boys if they were available. The Chief indicated he would talk with the tribal hunters and let them decide.

Finn glanced about him at the women in their rabbit-skinned blankets, evidently highly prized by the Maidu. Most of the huts were circular with inverted, cone-shaped roofs covered with leaves, mud, and a few animal skins. He noticed the many baskets with interesting patterns. He found out later that their baskets were made of peeled willows or peeled or unpeeled rosebud, and were always made in coils from their favorite woods.

Near the wide creek on the edge of the village, he saw several dugout canoes and a log raft, probably used for fishing.

He learned from Miles that the Maidu polished their money which consisted mostly of clam shells and disk beads. These were exchanged within and between tribes.

Two weeks later, as Bracken's health deteriorated, he asked an Indian boy working in the apple orchard to deliver a message to his son to come and get him. He said goodbye to Sean, and moved in with his children. Miles knew he would not make it much longer.

Before two months had passed, Sean received word of the old man's death.

Sean attended the funeral, feeling like he had lost a close friend. Miles' son told Sean that his father died due to the loss of his orchards, for they were his whole life.

Sean realized that his future rested in the hands of Miles Bracken's children, for they held the mortgage on Sean's property. Any miss-step on Sean's part, and Miles' children could take the property back.

Sean found he had inherited a sturdy, quality home and furnishings on the orchard property, and eagerly looked forward to getting his family relocated. There were five large bedrooms, kitchen with hand-pumped water, parlor or living room with a huge fireplace, and a large walkup attic for storage. Two outhouses were located in the rear of the home. The view from the wide covered front porch included all the orchards, the fruit storage barn, and tool-repair shed on the side full of numerous tools he could use; shears, clippers, saws, hammers, screwdrivers, wood planes, and hand drills. He would add his own tools to this collection. Attached to the shed, Sean saw the one-horse stable and hay loft for his horse, Martin. Sean smiled as he looked around him. With this orchard property, he and his family had moved up a notch. Now he had to make it produce and find plenty of customers.

He soon found himself using the third floor bedroom to read and meditate, where he could walk out on the balcony and survey his little kingdom at his leisure, and watch the sun set in the evenings. He felt at peace with the world and wanted his wife and son to share his good luck in finding this haven.

He got excited when he thought of Jennifer seeing this house for the first time.

He could hardly wait for that moment.

Chapter 3

March 1847

On days when not too busy, usually on Sunday, Sean explored the area around his new property, and especially Deer Creek less than five miles from his orchards. He planned to ride to the Maidu village as part of his exploration, but wanted to see Deer Creek near his new home. He had heard much about Deer Creek from Bracken. The sun rose as he approached the Creek with his fishing pole tied to one side of his saddle, and he dismounted, tied Martin to a small tree, untied his fishing pole, lifted a bucket from the saddle horn, and wandered down to the quietly flowing water. The creek appeared wide at this point, the flow meandered, and the water appeared to be five or six feet deep judging by the slope of the land on both sides of the creek. He watched an Indian boy swinging on a tree over the water while his friend watched and yelled. Sean smiled. Wouldn't mind doing that myself, he thought as he watched and heard them yelling to each other.

In a few minutes, Sean had his first fish. He didn't know what kind he had caught, but it looked like it might be good to eat. He put the fish in his small bucket with water and started to throw his line in again.

Suddenly, Sean heard a limb crack, and the scream of the young boy on the rope as the limb fell on top of him as he plummeted into the water. Sean watched in dread as the boy began to struggle in the water, the large limb on top of him, the rope tangled around the boy's arms and waist. Sean took off his shirt and removed his pants when he saw that the water covered the boy's head. Suddenly the limb dragged the boy under, his arms flailing, and he came up again choking and screaming, trying to inhale. The other boy dashed back and forth on the river bank, but did not know what to do. He appeared to be limping.

Sean quickly ran into the water in his underwear, swam strongly toward the drowning boy, yelling at them. The boy on the bank looked up, yelled, and waved his arms, and Sean saw that this boy had a deformed leg.

As he reached for the drowning boy, the tree limb dragged the boy under again and Sean dove under to find him.

Surprisingly, the water appeared deeper than Sean thought, but the water had murkiness, so Sean swam forward and moved his arms about until he felt the limb and found the boy in front of him. He grabbed him and struggled with the rope twisted around the boy. In panic the boy grabbed Sean around the neck and tried to climb up Sean's body to get to the surface. Sean finally wrenched free, grabbed the boy's arm, and swam for the surface, pushing the boy to the surface ahead of him. He came up next to the boy, who tried to inhale as he continued to slap at the water. Sean grabbed him from the rear, put his hand under the boy's chin, and swam toward shore.

He finally felt the river bottom under his feet, lifted the boy out of the water, and placed him on the ground as his friend limped over with terror on his face. The lame boy yelled and talked in a rapid language that Sean did not understand. Finally, the boy stopped talking, looked at Sean, and said in English, 'Me Ipsa.' The boy on the ground stopped coughing and lay still on the ground. Sean rolled him onto his stomach, turned his head to the side, and began to apply pressure on his lower back, trying to pump the water out of him. After a minute of pumping, the boy coughed roughly and spit out a mouthful of water, then lay sobbing on the ground, weak from his harrowing escape from drowning.

Sean saw the ponies the boys rode, and told Ipsa to ride for home. Ipsa did not understand, so Sean quickly drew an inverted 'V' like a tent or teepee. Ipsa looked curiously at the picture in the dirt, and pointed to the northeast.

Sean picked Ipsa up and set him on his horse. Then he picked up the unconscious boy and set him on the other horse, glanced toward his clothes and Martin on the far bank, mounted in his underwear, and cradled the boy in his arms as he shouted to Ipsa and waved him toward home.

The boy understood immediately and turned his pony northward. Sean followed, watching the boy's shallow breathing as they rode toward the boy's home. Ipsa constantly glanced back at Sean to be sure he followed. They rode north along the edge of the creek for about two miles, and then Ipsa turned away from the creek, yelled, and waved for Sean to follow.

Sean noticed that the creek widened here more than where he had swum across, and the water appeared shallow. He would have to remember this if he ever decided to bring his mule and wagon to the Maidu village. The spot looked familiar and he realized that Miles had made his crossing here when he brought him to the Indian village.

After another mile Sean saw the village ahead, round mud-and-log buildings, some partly covered with animal skins, all in irregular rows. As they entered the village, dogs barked and nipped at Sean's legs, and Ipsa yelled at them. Women peeked out of the huts, and watched as Sean rode into their camp. One woman screamed and ran to Sean's horse, grabbing for the boy in his arms. Sean handed him down as Ipsa slid off his horse and jabbered at the curious women who had formed a semi-circle around Sean's horse. Ipsa pointed at Sean several times. Sean slid off his horse and stood with his front toward the horse while he glanced around the village.

The woman took the boy into one of the huts and the others gathered around the entrance and watched, then turned to look at the white man. They seemed to be curious by his unclothed pale-skinned appearance.

Sean experienced total surprise when a young white woman came out of a large hut and approached him.

'What happened?' she asked.

Sean nodded toward the boy's hut. 'Thank God, someone is here who speaks English. A boy almost drowned in Deer Creek. A limb broke with the rope he swung on and he went in along with the limb. Got tangled up and I had to rescue him. Guess he doesn't know how to swim or maybe he just panicked.'

Sean felt embarrassed, for he stood in his undershorts, and tried to hide behind his horse. The young woman walked to the hut where the boy had been taken and talked in the Indian language. The woman came out holding the boy in her arms, and said something to Sean in her language.

The young woman translated. 'She wants to thank you for saving her son. She says if you need clothes, you can have the extra pants of her husband.'

'Yes, I could sure use clothes. Left mine on the river bank along with my horse. M'am, I'm Sean Kerry, the new owner of the Bracken orchards. I…'

'Oh, yes, I thought maybe you were Mr. Kerry. In fact, I planned to visit you soon to see how you were doing. Miles has a large orchard, and I figured you would be needing help with your harvests soon.'

Sean smiled in surprise. 'I couldn't have said it any better, Miss…"

'Hannah,' she said. 'Hannah Ehrens. Just call me Hannah. I live in Chico with my father. He's the blacksmith there.'

'I see. And you can call me Sean.'

She looked him up and down and smiled. 'Let me get those pants for you to wear, Sean. You look like a pale Indian right now.' She laughed, and the little group of women laughed and tittered also, not knowing what she laughed at.

Soon Sean had on cloth pants that were too big for him, and a loose cotton shirt, but at least they covered him. As Hannah led him to the Chief's hut, Sean watched her from behind as they walked–brilliant blonde hair, nice curves, about twenty years old. Too bad Finn couldn't see her. An enticing young woman, he thought. He especially noticed her attire, which differed drastically from that of his wife Jennifer with her full skirts, camisoles, corsets, and drawers.

Hannah had on knee-length boots of soft leather, maybe drawers or maybe not under her tan breeches, a light blue finger-tip-length jacket with puffed sleeves which fitted tight across her breasts and opened in front, held by three black buttons, no corset, he felt sure. Obviously, Hannah dressed for comfort, and had probably designed her outfit herself. She reminded Sean of a spirited tomboy.

Chief Sam's hut had a circular design, with a pointed roof covered with long leaves and soil, larger than the other huts. Around the periphery were dozens of varieties of wild flowers planted near the base,

Pincushion near the wall, cockscombs and daisies in front, and poppies in orange and yellow. The Chief's wife must like flowers, Sean thought. He noticed as he glanced around that many of the other huts had the same shape, but with fewer flowers.

Lucky for Sean, Hannah spoke the Indian dialect, a form of Penutian, she explained.

'The chief's name is Wah-She-Sam, but I call him Chief Sam for short and he doesn't seem to mind. The Maidu shy away from white men, so besides me, Miles Bracken was the only white man I've ever seen in the village, except for Doc Bryant from Chico, and he's only been here once.'

She spoke for a few moments to the Chief, and he nodded and grunted and stared at Sean with unhidden curiosity. Maybe without my clothes on, he doesn't remember meeting me before, he thought. Soon the Chief said something in his language and Hannah turned back to Sean.

'It seems that Miles Bracken exchanged flowers and fruits for help from the boys. But you ought to know that Miles always rewarded the boys who worked for him with toys, play guns like the white man uses, small knives, hatchets, steel tips for their arrows, tools for their fathers, and lots of candy.' She laughed again and her eyes twinkled.

'Figure out how many boys you can use and let me know when you need them and the chief will see that you have your help. I think Miles Bracken employed about eight or nine boys at a time. Most of the Yamadi Maidu men are off hunting right now, but you will probably see them soon. They will be naturally curious to see a white man, since so few ever show up here in the village, and the Maidu are hesitant about dealing with white men in general. You will probably be one of their exceptions since you will give them fruits like Miles did.

'By the way, Sean, I have an agenda with the Maidu, too. I am trying to teach the boys English, and I have one or two students who may be helpful to you if you want to learn to speak their language.'

'Oh, and one more thing while we're at it. I am trying to convince the Maidu to grow their own food. But I get a lot of opposition since the Maidu are hunters and rather nomadic. They say they don't have time or the means to be tending to gardens and such. And I have no extra funds to spend on garden tools for them, so I have my work cut out for me.'

She shrugged her shoulders and glanced at him over her shoulder. 'I also have several health issues I discuss with them from time to time, but they are so set in their ways that I don't seem to get through to them. One tribe of the Washoe Indians on the Sacramento River has been decimated by small pox because the Indians have not been inoculated against white men's diseases like small pox and cholera.'

Sean took her comment about growing their own food as a request if he were so inclined, and he could see how supplying the Maidu with the means to plow a field might help him in his quest for help in his orchards in the future. He thought a trip to Chico might be in order now that he felt settled in waiting for Jennifer. Once he saw that the boy he had saved moved about, Sean rode behind an Indian boy, waved farewell to Hannah and Chief Sam and made his way back to pick up his horse, clothes, fishing pole, and bucket with the fish on the river bank, and then headed home on Martin.

He had agreed to meet Hannah in Chico so they could pick up a plow, harness, and a mule for the Maidu Indians.

For some reason all Sean could think about was meeting Hannah Ehrens again. She was a hard woman to forget.

Chapter 4

April – August 1847

Three days later Sean made his way to the Maidu village again with Hannah Ehrens beside him in the wagon, with a mule tied behind, and a plow and harness in the wagon bed. As they entered the village this time, many of the men were home from their hunt and soon gathered around his wagon to inspect the plow and harness. Two of them ran their hands over the mule and inspected his teeth.

Soon they were laughing and offered Sean a drink of some type of spirits. His first taste made his eyes water, and the men laughed. Hannah joined the women and they soon had their own spirits circulating in a group near the creek.

After a while, Hannah approached Chief Sam who spoke tolerable English, and Sean listened.

'Chief Sam, remember we talked about vaccinating your tribe against smallpox and cholera? I have made arrangements with Dr. Bryant in Chico, and he believes he now has enough serum to vaccinate your whole tribe. Almost a complete village of the Washoe at Lake Tahoe died because of smallpox recently. I urge you to consider vaccination for your people as soon as possible. All white people are vaccinated.'

The Chief held up his hand.

'I have talked to my people about this white man medicine. None of the mothers and fathers is willing to be vaccinated; however, we will allow the children to be vaccinated if the parents wish.'

Hannah listened solemnly and replied.

'But Dr. Bryant has enough serum to inoculate your whole tribe, not just the children…'

'I have spoken. You can have the children vaccinated.' He sat down and picked up his glass, ignoring her. Sean could see that she wanted to say more. An interesting woman, Sean thought – a woman with an agenda, and always eager to help the Maidu, but definitely challenged by years of Maidu culture separated from the white man.

Hannah glared at the Chief's back and finally shrugged her shoulders.

Sean asked, 'Hannah, will Dr. Bryant come here to the Maidu village for the vaccinations?'

'Yes, he has been here before to discuss sanitation with Chief Sam. Their fecal habits leave much to be desired. After a season, they usually move their village a mile or so to get away from the smell. It's difficult to get them to change their ways. They have terrible sanitation conditions.'

She went back to the women and Sean continued talking to the men. After a while the men brought their sons to Sean so he could choose help for his orchards. Realizing that being chosen might be an honor in the Maidu way of thinking, first Sean asked which boys would be interested in picking fruit and learning about handling fruits. Twelve boys stepped forward with their fathers urging them forward. He could see that this could be a source of pride for the fathers, so Sean took his time and chose more boys than he could use because he didn't want anyone to feel slighted or left out.

Eventually, he had selected eight boys who had worked for Bracken in the past, and seemed interested in helping with Sean's harvests, including the little lame boy, Ipsa, whose face beamed when Sean chose him. He also included a young giant with a muscular build named Oakum who Sean could see would be a great help in the orchards.

In no time, Hannah and the Maidu women had prepared a small feast and Sean could not decline their invitation, for he had eaten their venison stew after the women showed him how to prepare it, and he always looked forward to another helping.

His main difficulty consisted of making himself understood. He knew he would have to learn their language immediately if he were to make friends with these sturdy Indians. Having Hannah with him became a great advantage in getting his ideas across. Perhaps she would

33

help him with the language, too. He watched her from the other side of the feast, her fair hair blowing in the breeze, and her animated voice carrying above the voices of the Indians.

A gorgeous young woman, Sean decided, as he glanced over at her. His own desires stirred, he felt she would make some young man a fine wife. He had to be sure to get Hannah and Finn together at every excuse, for they looked like a good match, both interested in progress, healthy lifestyles, and especially fruit-growing. On several occasions, Sean caught Hannah watching him, and smiled in return. She would look away quickly as if embarrassed. Sean didn't know what to make of her actions, and concentrated on his food.

Sean knew that Hannah Ehrens also tried to teach the Washoe to farm the fertile valleys to the West of the Sacramento River, but they, like the Maidu, were reluctant to put their faith in growing their own food, for they were hunters.

The Washoe refused to consider farming, since in their culture, they were nomadic by nature, and refused to be tied to one place to tend plant growth. From Hannah's description of the Washoe and their ways, Hannah convinced Sean that he could find no help for his harvests from the Washoe tribe, not to mention that they lived farther away than the Maidu.

Sean listened as Hannah tried to convince the Maidu women to plant and harvest corn. The men were definitely not interested, so Hannah directed her efforts to the women who were always more receptive to new ideas.

She explained in their language about planting corn.

'Do not try to plant corn until after the last frost or seeds will rot. You must plant every few weeks from early May to July to get corn continuously during the growing season. Plant 10-15 seeds per person—for 60 Indians, that's 600 to 900 seeds. I will try to get seeds for you from Jon Simms' store in Chico. He may give me a price break on the seed if he knows they are for you.

'Plant seeds in groups of 3 to be sure at least one will grow. Corn needs full sun, and must be free of weeds.

The ground should be well fertilized 2-3 weeks before planting. Plant 1-2 inches below the surface, and space the plants about 30 inches apart.

'You must water one inch per week at ground level, not on the plant. Tassels will appear usually at knee level—they are like yellow strands of hair.

'The corn should be finished growing 3 weeks after tassels appear. You can eat as you pick the ears, or boil the ears for 10 to 15 minutes, butter, and serve...oh, that's right, you don't have butter.' She brightened. 'But corn is good simply boiled and salted.'

Hannah watched the women as she talked. Some listened half-heartedly, some dozed, and one or two listened attentively. She glanced at Sean Kerry, looked up toward the sky, and shrugged.

Sean beckoned her over.

'Hannah, I think you're telling the wrong people. The adults are too set in their ways. You should give this lecture to the boys and girls. They are more ready to accept a new idea. Try it; maybe start with the boys while they eat lunch at the orchards. You may be surprised at the results. I have a few boys who are already asking me about starting their own orchards. I think you'd have a much better chance with them.'

She listened, nodded, and said, 'Maybe you're right, Sean. I'll have to give it a try some day when I visit your orchards.'

Chapter 5

September 1847

When they left the village with her chestnut horse tied to the back of his wagon, Sean knew it would be a long ride to Chico, so he invited Hannah to stop off at his place and have lunch. She agreed readily, and they talked of their projects and how the Maidu were reacting to their teaching.

Before long they were at Sean's home, and Hannah took charge and made them a lunch of venison stew which Sean had saved, mixed in bacon, and made a small salad from his partly-eaten head of lettuce. Sean pumped cool water from the sink, added lemon and sugar, and set two full glasses on the table.

'Sean, let's eat on your front porch. The view is magnificent from there.'

Before they realized it, an hour had slipped by as they talked, and the sun had begun to set.

'While I'm here, would you show me your house? I've never seen more than the porch when Miles owned the place.'

Sean, more than happy to show off his beautiful home, took her through the entire downstairs, and paused, looking at her with curiosity.

'I guess you've seen bedrooms before. We have five of them upstairs, and they're large...'

She rested her hand on his arm.

'Would you show them to me, Sean? I'd like to see them. I'll even take my boots off so I don't spoil your rugs.'

Sean looked at her, and his pulse rose. He stepped away from her and studied her for a moment as she sat down and held out her leg toward him. He turned, straddled her booted leg, and, while she pushed on his rear, he pulled the boot off. Then he did the same with the other one. Her touch sent shivers up his spine.

Of course, he lied to himself; she may not have seen a house this large before. And she tried to be neat and not soil his carpets upstairs. As she led him to the steps, his thoughts were jumbled, and he felt his heart beat harder. He knew he should be calm, for after all, they were just bedrooms.

Within five minutes he had shown her three of the bedrooms and then they arrived at the fourth. This one consisted of the turret room high on the third floor, all by itself which had a wide balcony that overlooked the whole property.

'In fact,' he said, 'you can see Deer Creek if you look closely.' They stood at the doorway almost touching. Did he feel heat coming from her arms, or was that his imagination? He wondered.

'And this is where I come when I want to read late at night, where I can look out at the orchards and…'

Her arm rested on his again and her hand touched the back of his hand.

'I…Hannah, are you sure you want to see this last room? I mean, it's only a bedroom.'

'But it's one of *your* bedrooms, Sean, and I want to see where you might sleep. Can I see it? Please?' she begged in a low, velvety voice.

He opened the door and before he realized, she glided past him, arms rising as she twirled around several times, darted to the balcony, stood leaning over the balcony provocatively, looked at the view for a few moments, posing in the fading light, tip-toed back into the room, and lay on the bed, holding out her arms to him in a tantalizing way.

'Come, join me, Sean. I know you want to. And I want you to…I've thought of nothing else since I met you.'

'Hannah, we can't…Hannah, I'm a married man. I can't…you shouldn't…'

But Hannah had unbuttoned her blue jacket, taken it off, and dropped it by the side of the bed. Next came her belt, shoulder straps and breeches which also dropped over the side of the bed, and Sean stood beyond help as he watched her undress, partly torn by guilt in his desire, but unable to pull himself out of the moment.

She had no camisole under the jacket and no corset as he had guessed.

'Would you help me with these?'

He hesitated for an instant, but in seconds helped her off with her drawers, and then he fumbled out of his own clothes, and she rose to help him, while he scanned her up and down with wide eyes. She lay back, pulling him down with her, he melted into her arms, and the rest fogged in his mind. They did things he had never dreamed of before and soon he found himself mesmerized by this delicious woman.

An hour later she was dressed and sitting on the porch swing next to him, her arms around his neck, her head tucked into his shoulder.

'I know I took you by surprise, Sean, but I've watched you every time we've been thrown together, and I've seen how you look at me. I don't think I could ever have done this with another man. Honest. The truth is I feel the same about you. Does that shock you? I think I'm in love with you, Sean.'

He was quiet all the way to Chico as he drove her home. His mind was in turmoil, and he didn't know what to do since they had made love. She clung to him softly until they reached the outskirts of town, and then sat up prim and straight as he drove to her house, untied her horse, and handed her the reins.

He rode home in a cloud, a dark cloud. What had he done? He wondered. This must never happen again.

Chapter 6

October 1847

In October 1847, orchardist Sean Kerry surveyed the Yamadi Maidu Indian village as he drove his wagon into the compound with bushels of fruit for them, little enough payment for the orchard help they provided with the Indian boys.

Hannah Ehrens stood in the middle of a crowd of Indian boys, talking to them about planting their own crops, her bright golden hair blowing in the breeze, her Tomboy, but feminine shape, making his pulse rise as he watched the beautiful young girl trying to help the Maidu Indians.

Hannah saw him as Sean jumped from his wagon, and she walked over.

'You were right, Sean. The boys took to the idea of growing their own corn right off. I can't believe it. They actually have a small cornfield planted and growing, and I noticed some of the mothers and fathers watching the fields, too. Many of them have been asking me questions. Oh, if only this will work for the Maidu. Of course, I realize that this is a bit late to be planting corn, but at least they will get some experience. I told them that they must plant in early May, but they insisted on trying anyway. I hope out-of-season planting like this doesn't sour them on planting corn next May.'

Sean watched her with pleasure. It satisfied him to see her bubbling enthusiasm.

He remembered that first night with Hannah in his bed, the night she surprised and seduced him, and his pulse quickened as he relived the night again. At forty-six, he still felt amazed that a beautiful woman like Hannah would be drawn to him, a married man.

He tried to clarify his thinking and watched her as they sat around the fire with the Maidu. Finally, his attention was redirected toward the flashes of yellow light from the Maidu women's jewelry.

As they ate in the clearing while sitting on the ground, Sean noticed that today, many of the Maidu women wore bracelets, necklaces, and even ankle bracelets of small, shiny yellow stones. This was the first time he noticed this jewelry. Evidently they didn't wear it often. Sean studied the stones subtly and wondered, could these stones be gold? Did the Maidu have a source of gold somewhere in the area? Were the women beginning to trust him even though he was a white man and an outsider?

He pointed to one of the bracelets the woman near him wore. She raised her arm in a question and pointed at her bracelet. Sean nodded, and she removed the bracelet and handed it to him. Sean studied the various-sized stones on the bracelet closely and decided this jewelry was pure gold in the form of small smoothed nuggets. He handed the woman her bracelet and thanked her, and then proceeded to eat his food without further comment. He decided if gold existed around here, he had to approach the subject carefully with the Maidu. He noticed that several of the boys wore necklaces with a single nugget, and decided that eventually he would ask the boys who worked in his orchards about the gold.

For now he was content to have all the help he needed from the Maidu tribe, and didn't want to jeopardize it with a typical white man's greed. He didn't need gold, he thought, and all of the problems it might bring.

He tried to concentrate on how to teach the boys about growing his fruits, for most of them were still hunters like their fathers.

Sean found himself with four types of orchards: with 30 acres of apples and 20 acres of apricots, plus 10 acres each of plums and pears, using all but about 15 acres of the eighty-five acres in his possession.

He wanted to pique the interest of the Maidu boys and get them to like growing plants as he did.

During a normal day, Sean was up early, had oatmeal and coffee, and was soon engrossed in the work of the orchards. Many days he would get so involved, he would forget to eat lunch, unless the Indian boys reminded him.

Until his wife, Jennifer, arrived from Wadsworth, Nevada, his food consisted of cornmeal, flour, bacon slabs, eggs, milk, sugar, and salt, since he was alone for several months. He simply had no time to fix fine meals. But he did eat his own fruit.

Initially Sean sold his fruit in Chico, California and sometimes in other small towns along the Sacramento River and Deer Creek near his new orchards. He would display his fruits in front of a local store and often sit in a chair, wait for customers, and watch the people go by. He soon began to know some of the people who stopped by his fruit displays to talk.

Sean found that many of his customers allowed for a blemish or two on the fruits he sold them, so he did not consider himself a purist when it came to the caliber of his fruit, but he continually strived to grow the best and healthiest fruit possible, and would hand-pick fruits for his best customers.

In Nevada, Sean's home and orchards were located in a valley outside Wadsworth, Nevada. He had made agreements with most of the local stores to sell his fruits, but he had no such agreements here and there was only Jon Simm's store in Chico at first. Later he found that Chico had more stores and they were more than willing to handle his fruits since his was one of only a few orchards in the area.

With Sean's new 85-acre property, he needed help tending this large orchard. He had about 80 trees per acre in a loose planting arrangement, but in a grid system.

He remembered his father's old saying: 'Keep using the same practices on your fruit trees and the results will remain the same.' In other words, his father told him to do everything in his power to increase the fruit tree yield, fruit tree height, and fruit size.

The tree height in his orchards due to the efforts of Miles Bracken, the previous owner, was outstanding:

Apple trees grew to 25 feet; apricot to 20 feet; plums to 30 feet; pears to 40 feet. Ladders were used to harvest all varieties of fruit.

Miles Bracken planted his trees at a distance between trees roughly equal to their height.

Sean knew he must prune his trees annually to shape them and promote healthy growth. He remembered that fateful spring when the leaves turned black, shriveled, as if burned by fire, limbs became brittle, and the bark dried out on his trees in Nevada. That was the beginning of the end of his old orchards.

He couldn't wait to teach the boys about pruning.

Sean found that climbing into most of his trees was easy. The Indian boys had each picked a favorite tree limb to sit on while eating their lunch of jerky or whatever Sean provided.

Sean trained the boys who were willing to learn the ways of the orchard; some stayed to work with him, others wanted to hunt as their fathers did.

Early one morning soon after the meeting at the Maidu village, the eight boys arrived two to a pony eager to help Sean with his fruits. They began calling him 'Fruit Chief' in their language, and as this seemed appropriate, Sean accepted it.

While the boys worked in the orchards, Sean spliced fruit varieties in the experimental orchard by cutting a diagonal on the limb of a new variety, and then a similar cut on an existing limb, joined them tightly together, and wrapped them in a splint of wet cloth.

Daily Sean would walk the rows of his fruit trees, appraising the health of the fruit. He could tell just by rubbing his fingers lightly over the bark and limbs and fruit surfaces if his fruits were healthy. To him touching the fruit was like caressing a beautiful woman.

He used bee-keeping in order to pollinate certain of his fruit trees, locating them near the orchards and taking advantage of the numerous flowers appearing in spring for pollen and honey.

Luckily, apricots were self-pollinating so the small apricot orchard had survived in Wadsworth, Nevada and provided a bit of income for his wife while he searched out new orchards for his family in California.

In this group of Maidu Indians one boy spoke broken English, the Chief's son, Ruma.

Sean sat down with the boys in the shade and through Ruma explained to them all about growing fruit and the many side issues that they must learn in order to keep the orchards healthy.

Sean looked at the harvest schedule Miles had made for him before he left.

Jan-Feb	Apples
May-July	Apricots
May-Sep	Plums
Aug-Nov	Apples
Oct-Dec	Pears

Through Ruma he explained the various fruits to them and had them say the name of the fruit as he passed pieces of each fruit among them. By showing them his harvest schedule, they could see that they would be helping Fruit Chief on and off all year.

Sean explained to the boys how he adhered to growing principles he had lived by most of his life, and told them about a few new ones supplied by Miles Bracken, the sharp old orchardist who preceded him in these orchards.

'In your Kuksu religion, the men, through rituals and secret dances, pray to a higher spirit for good health, bountiful harvests of acorns from the oak trees, good hunts, fertility, and good weather. Chief Sam explained these things to me.

'In my religion, my higher spirit is called God. I believe that Nature is a tool of *my* God, and He places a bit of Himself in every plant and fruit on earth through the use of Nature. So I try to use God's tools to grow healthy fruits so that everyone can eat, taste, and enjoy the sweetness of God.'

He taught the Indian boys to plant and tend the young trees or saplings, teaching them how to splice limbs of different varieties in his experimental area. He built wooden frames to support young trees, and showed several of the boys how to make these frames and install them.

One boy in particular, Ruma, son of Chief Sam always seemed to be more interested in fruit growing than the rest, and Sean began to train him in the ways of his fruit orchards.

'I believe in growing food for my people,' said Ruma. 'A Chief must do all possible to make sure his people do not grow hungry. That is why we take care of the oak trees, so that we can have acorns in the winter. Growing fruit like you do is same thing. And there are other plants that are good for eating. Hannah Ehrens has shown us how to plant corn and tomatoes and beans. This is good. Along with the meats from our hunts, we have a good food mixture. She is having trouble convincing the elders of my tribe to grow their own food, but I listen well, for this may be our salvation some day.'

Eventually, he made Ruma the leader of the team of boys and let him direct operations on one or two of the orchards. Ruma reminded Sean of Finn, with his love for growing things.

Most of Sean's orchards were planted in a grid, making the work easier at harvest time and pruning time, and for irrigation purposes. And he liked to improve the esthetics of his orchards, so he showed the boys the art of planting flowers randomly around the orchards, and benches where one could sit and enjoy the beauty of the growing fruit. The boys liked this idea, for their mothers used such ideas around their homes.

On days when there was not a lot of work in the orchard, the boys would hunt with bows and arrows and bring fresh venison to Sean and even a deer hide on occasion, while he shared his biscuits and other food with them at lunch. Their mothers showed Sean how to make tasty venison stew. The boys had been bringing their fathers to the Kerry Orchards due to the great number of deer who also liked Sean's fruits, and the boys would tow their fathers around from tree to tree and fruit to fruit to show them what they were doing.

Sean always had plenty of ground coffee on hand, and would make biscuits when he had the time. Since he was generally frugal by nature, he kept one mule and one horse, and used the mule to pull his wagon to the markets in Chico, and on occasion to markets in other towns.

Sean then took the boys into the orchard and showed them how to prune a tree limb.

'We will practice pruning later when pruning is necessary, and I will show you several methods of pruning which help to grow better fruit by allowing fruits in the center to get more sun. Sunlight is important to a growing plant.'

By the first of May the plum and apricot harvests were underway; by this time Sean had trained the boys well in the methods of picking and handling the fruits. They were all good workers and never seemed to tire; their handling of the fruit and trees was more than Sean could have hoped for, and Sean was delighted at this excellent source of help – at such a reasonable price.

He could see that several of the boys were greatly interested in growing fruit, and he began to think about a small orchard near their home village where the boys could practice growing trees. He knew that once they began, they would soon overwhelm him with questions. And he knew that was good. It would show their level of interest.

His only problem so far was with the boy, Oakum, a young giant of a boy about seven feet tall and powerful, but extremely accident-prone. He dropped boxes of fruits, tripped over his own feet, upset ladders resting on trees, and once through his clumsiness broke one of the clay pipes in an irrigation row. He caused Sean extra work. Sean knew that he would have to exclude Oakum from the group unless he could find some simple task that would keep him out of the way of the harvest. He could always use his strength on occasion, but must keep him away from the fruit picking and handling. Eventually he made him their water boy, and allowed him to carry water to the boys as they worked, but always in the center of tree rows away from the clay irrigation pipes.

His wagon was full of wooden boxes of plums and apricots for the third time in nine days, and he saw that this was the last wagon-load he would take to Chico where he had made contracts with seven local stores to sell his fruits. He bartered at the local Chico stores, offering his fruits in exchange for his normally needed supplies: wood, tools, sacking material, and food. Their percentages from sales of his fruits were reasonable and Sean felt good about the relationship. He also bartered with Jon Simms to get grafts of new species on occasion and grafted them to healthy trees in his experimental area. He was on the mailing list of several seed catalogs, and soon had a stack of seed and plant catalogs which he continually perused in his evening hours after the orchard work.

He found that new varieties grafted to full-grown trees produced fruit in one to two seasons as compared to the many years required to plant and nurture a new variety of tree to maturity from saplings. He was able to incorporate new varieties into his orchards quickly.

In his reading about fruit trees, Sean had picked up some tips from William Cox from his book, *A View of the Cultivation of fruit trees.* He put this knowledge together with what Miles Bracken and his own father had taught him for healthy orchards and a highly successful orchard business.

He learned that the color of the fruit has no correlation to tree diseases.

And skin thickness may be a factor in tree disease since insects have a harder time getting to the fruit with tough skins, so Sean experimented to cull out thin-skinned fruits.

Whitewashing the lower trunks of fruit trees helped avoid insects.

He felt contented with his orchards and what he knew, but he also knew that he must continue to learn more and keep learning in order to have the best fruit orchards in California.

Chapter 7

August 1847

Jennifer had written that she was finally packed and ready to make the trip to their new home. Sean made arrangements with Mort Persons at the livery stables to transport his wife and furniture to the Kerry Orchards as soon as she arrived in Chico. He was eager as a young boy for her to see their new home.

At the end of work the next day, he thanked the boys and they relaxed in the shade before Sean made the next trip. He reached under the seat of the wagon and pulled out a bag of rewards for the boys. He spread the contents on the ground and told them to pick any item they liked. Sean had lead soldiers and Indians, play guns, small knives, hatchets, steel arrow heads, plus several tools for their fathers, cloth and buttons for their mothers, and a small mound of toffee candy.

Sean was proud of his increasing command of their language, for the boys had been teaching him daily for many weeks during the harvest when Sean climbed into the trees with the boys, picked fruit and handled it gently as always to set a good example for the boys in the process. He also taught them English as they worked, and they seemed to be picking up many English words.

'Here are some of the guidelines I adhere to in growing fruits in my orchards. Don't try to remember all of them now. We will practice using these guidelines as we work.

'Always water the trees early in the day to limit evaporation'. He had to explain words like 'evaporation' until they understood.

'An irrigation pond like the one here can be managed so that water is always available for the trees – filled from a larger water source from nearby Deer Creek.' The word 'irrigation' took a while to get across. 'It means to supply water to an area.' They finally understood.

'Fruit trees grow well if irrigated and pruned regularly; low water at roots means leaves will wilt, curl, and sunburn. It's easy to keep an eye on this…'

'What is 'prune', Fruit Chief?' asked the Indian boy, Ipsa, and Sean explained with examples on a broken limb by trimming off a shriveled leaf with his hand shears.

'Too little water brings on what my father called 'fruit tree blues' which limits the size and taste of fruit; however, a slight reduction in water at specific growth stages can improve fruit flavor, add sugar and oil content, and limit vegetation growth near the trees…'

He watched as they glanced at one another with confusion written on their faces.

'As I said, don't try to understand everything I am telling you at once. We will discuss these things more as we work with the fruits and trees.

'And here's another important thing. Always have good drainage; do not let water 'pool' near trees.' Again he explained good runoff so that water did not sit in pockets in the soil.

'The best orchard is like those you see here; located on a slight rise or fall for easy water flow to all trees by gravity.' It took Sean a while before he could explain 'gravity'. In the case of water, gravity caused water to flow from a high place to a low place until it can go no further.

'Irrigate thoroughly, but not frequently. The key is to know how much water to use and how often. You can tell by the color and feel of the leaves.'

'Irrigation simply means supplying water to your plants. In the spring and fall, trees need less water, but always start irrigating in early spring.

'The amount of water a fruit tree uses depends on how big the tree is and how hot the weather. The goal is always to get the most growth early in a tree's life.

'Most fruit tree varieties need about 15-19 gals per day.' Here he showed them a gallon bucket and showed them by counting how many buckets of water 'fifteen' was. All the boys were surprised that trees needed so much water.

'Leaves should cover the outside area the same for most species of fruit trees.' He showed them a ball and compared it to the shape of a tree. This they understood.

'Drip irrigation is good, as it only wets a small area and limits weed growth near the trees.'

Although many of the boys had worked for Miles Bracken in the past, Miles had evidently not explained in detail about the maintenance of a fruit orchard, and they were still curious about the clay pipe and the drip irrigation. In fact, many of the boys were curious about everything Sean did in his orchards and were continually asking questions.

'Trees with one one-gallon drip on each side need to be irrigated 8-9 hours every day if conditions are dry, otherwise, once per day. That's from just after sun rise to just before sun set. Or you can do it the other way around; irrigate from sunset to sunrise.'

'An orchard's worst enemy is spring frost and lack of irrigation. These concerns are minimal in Kerry valley where my orchards are. I have plenty of water and usually mild winters with few frosts.'

As they rested in the shade, Sean pointed to the nugget on a leather thong hanging from the neck of one of the boys. The boy smiled proudly, took off the necklace, and handed it to Sean. This was the largest nugget Sean had seen so far, and he told the boys of his interest in the yellow stones. They looked at him with surprise, glanced at one another, and laughed.

Sean asked them what was funny, and Ruma, the oldest boy, explained.

'We have lots of these yellow stones of every size, and they are easy to get, but they are good for nothing besides jewelry, mostly for the women, although many of the boys also wear small nuggets on thongs around their neck like this one that their mothers made for them.'

'Our fathers warn us against wearing any of this jewelry among white men, for they know about the curious wants and greed of whites. The Maidu men and women strive to protect their culture and heritage, and stay away from the white man's world as much as possible. Hannah, Dr. Bryant, and you, Fruit Chief, are the only ones he trusts.

'But why would Fruit Chief want these sun-colored stones?' he asked.

'What good are they?'

'In the white man's world where I live, these yellow stones are considered valuable, but you should not show these stones to other white man, or bad things may happen to your people when the white prospectors begin to scour the creeks and rivers around your homes.

'They might ruin your water supply and perhaps bring white man diseases among your people. Your way of life is good and will remain so as long as you protect your culture from outside forces.'

Ruma nodded. 'Yes, our fathers have warned us about white men in Chico; they are greedy and do not treat the Maidu well. But my father, the Chief, likes you since you give us good fruits and trade good things to boys.'

Sean asks them where they get the nuggets, but they glanced at each other and remained silent. Obviously, they were not willing to tell him, for they had been indoctrinated by their fathers and their culture to be suspicious of white men, and do not fully trust Sean the Fruit Chief yet; however, they seem as if they want to tell him, but their Chief's warning held them back.

'Never mind, boys. Forget I asked. It's not important to me. I was just curious.'

Ruma conferred with the other boys, and finally approached Sean.

'You good to Maidu, Fruit Chief. My mother like you, my father like you. He has a bad feel for white man because they treat Maidu bad. Maybe one day we show. Tomorrow we bring yellow stones for you. You like?'

Sean shrugged his shoulders and chuckled. 'If you want. I have no real need for these yellow stones now. Sure, bring me a few nuggets. That's good enough for me, Ruma. You are all good boys, and I will trade with you for any yellow stones or gold dust you bring me. Let's leave it like that. What kinds of things would you like me to trade with you?'

Ruma once again conferred with the other boys, and much shouting and waving of hands took place. Finally, Ruma held up his hand, and the talk stopped. Sean snickered as he realized he saw a Chief-in-the-making in Ruma. He turned to Sean. 'Ruma like steel arrow heads, Ipsa like knives, Geno like shoes like you, but the rest no care… mothers say gifts from Fruit Chief good medicine; maybe something for mothers. They like shiny things, soft cloth, and buttons. And fathers like metal tools.'

Sean nodded. 'Okay, come tomorrow and we'll clean up the orchard and prepare for the apples in August…the yellow and red leaf season. What is your word for August?'

Ruma said, 'Tem-simi.'

Sean repeated the word aloud, and then said it to himself several times—Tem-simi is August, Tem-simi is August.

Within minutes, the boys had mounted their ponies, waved, and were off for home.

Soon after the boys departed, a heavily loaded wagon came up the road and he recognized Jennifer's chestnut hair as she sat on the seat next to the livery stable owner, Mort Persons and his helper. Jennifer waved excitedly with one hand as she held on to the wagon seat with the other as the loaded wagon swayed and bounced over the rough road.

She stepped down from the wagon and ran to Sean with arms wide, and Sean thought, my beautiful, wonderful wife. Sean embraced her tenderly, and kissed her as if they had just become lovers.

Jennifer looked up at the house and put her hands to her mouth.

'I…Oh, Sean. The house is beautiful beyond my wildest dreams. Why, it's twice the size of our Wadsworth home.'

'Oh, Jenn. Now that you're here, my life's complete,' he said and threw his arms about her, and then grabbed her hand and pulled her up the porch steps.

'Wait'll you see the inside, Jenn. You're going to love the kitchen; it has a water pump built in by the kitchen sink. And wait'll you see the fireplace. It's huge.'

Mort Persons helped them unload their possessions from the wagon, and Sean offered him dinner, but he declined. In less than an hour he was headed back to Chico. Jennifer waved to him.

'The people here are so friendly, Sean. I guess I worried for no reason. I'm sure I can get comfortable here in a short time. But I'll always miss our Wadsworth neighbors.'

Once Jennifer saw the kitchen, she immediately unpacked kitchen items and soon made the first real dinner Sean had in months.

As he showed her to their bedroom, Jennifer hugged him again.

'I'm so glad to be home at last.'

He smiled and kissed her.

'So am I, Jenn. With you here, this is finally home for me.

'But what about Finn? How soon will be joining us?'

Jennifer looked glum for a moment.

'He says he has about two more months on his book and then he'll be here. He still has lots of editing to do.'

Three days later after the work in the orchard was finished for the day, the boys followed Sean up to the house for a cold drink. They were already getting familiar with Jennifer's lemonade, and so they sat on the steps and enjoyed the cool sweet drink. They had adopted her as the 'Fruit Queen', and she felt pleased that they included her in their thinking.

Sean came out of the house and sat on the porch swing, put his feet up, and crossed his legs. He produced his metal flute and began to play music, and the boys turned to him in surprise and listened in awe.

'It's been so long since I heard you play in the evenings. At our old place, you used to play it almost every night.'

He winked at her and played for about a half hour and finally put down the flute. Immediately the boys gathered around him and wanted to see this great instrument.

Ruma said, 'Our fathers have four-holed flutes, but their music is nowhere near as nice and clear as yours.

After they left, Sean decided to show them how to make their own flutes.

Chapter 8

September 1847

The next day as Sean sat on his porch and waited for the boys, and Jennifer worked on a quilt in the living room with all the windows open, he saw four unshod Indian ponies approaching with two Indian boys on each pony as before. They had no saddles and only ropes to guide the horses. Each boy clutched something in his hands that looked like a lunch bag.

The boys slid off their horses and sat on the porch steps, each with a small animal skin bag in hand. Ruma handed Sean a small bag, and when Sean took it, the weight surprised him.

'Wait. Let me get a table cloth from Jenn so the gold dust won't fall through. He returned with a small square cloth, poured out the contents, and stood staring at the small gold nuggets. He estimated the weight of shiny yellow stones at about 2 pounds. He looked in amazement and thought, at over twenty dollars per ounce, that's…over six hundred dollars! And all from one little bag!

'Ruma,' Sean said, 'is this bag from all of you?'

They glanced at each other and laughed.

'No,' Ruma said. 'Each boy has a bag for you from his mother and father, Fruit Chief.'

Sean looked at them in disbelief.

'But boys, don't your parents realize the value of these nuggets? Are you sure your mothers and fathers would want you to give these to me?'

'Yes, we are sure. Take, please.'

'Hold it, Ruma. Let me get a pencil and paper and a fruit balance scale so I can keep track of each bagful of nuggets...stones, and who owns the bag. I may have to give these back to you after I speak with Chief Sam.'

He ran into the house and came out with paper and pencil, then walked to the shed, and came back with a balance scale used for weighing baskets of fruit. Lead weights hung from a rod along the side. The boys watched with curiosity as Sean began to write on the paper. The lame boy, Ipsa, reached out and touched the paper, then rubbed his fingers over the surface. He smiled at Sean and held out his bag.

'Let me weigh Ruma's bag first, Ipsa.' Sean gathered Ruma's nuggets, dumped the contents in the scale bowl, and added lead weights until the scale balanced. He added the weights and realized that Ruma's bagful weighed two pounds.

Sean collapsed into his rocker and looked quizzically at the eight boys.

'Lads, are you sure you want to give me all these nuggets? Do your mothers and fathers know you are giving me these stones? I wouldn't want to do anything against the Maidu tribe. In the white man's world these are worth a lot of money. They can buy many good things; clothes for your mother and father, food, cured animal skins, flint and steel for starting fires, shoes for men, women, and boys, and many other things.'

Ipsa stood proudly. 'My mother gave me smallest of her yellow stones and said give to Fruit Chief, and my father shook his head yes.'

Sean shook his head. By the time he had emptied all eight bags, he figured the average weight per bag was about 2 pounds! He did a few calculations. He was looking at almost fifty-three hundred dollars in gold! Sean felt guilty about accepting all this gold. He must talk again with the fathers and make them understand the value of these gold nuggets in the white man's world.

Sean went into the house, told Jennifer to come out to the porch, and showed her the gold. All she could do is stare in amazement. Sean brought out a large wicker basket full of toys, steel arrow heads, knives, hatchets, two pair of boy-sized shoes plus tools for the fathers, and cloth and buttons for the women. The boys dove into the basket, picking out their favorite items and holding them against their chests possessively.

The most any boy took was two items.

'Jenn, look at this gold! Each boy has brought me an average of two pounds of gold nuggets; that's sixteen pounds. At $20.67 an ounce, that's almost fifty-three hundred dollars from all eight boys.'

'Sean Kerry, have you talked to the Maidu men and made them understand the value of these nuggets? I can't believe they would simply give you that much gold.'

'Jenn, gold is not a thing of value in their society. The women use them for trinkets, necklaces, and ankle bracelets, and a few of the boys wear a nugget on a thong around their necks, but that's about it. I explained how valuable this gold is to a white man, and their reply is that they are happy that we are happy with these yellow stones. No white man has ever seen these yellow stones before us. They won't talk to other white men about this, and the women never wear their jewelry outside the village or in front of strangers. Hannah is the only white person to ever see this jewelry, and I don't think she is aware that these nuggets are gold. But I will talk to her also, to make sure she doesn't tell anyone there is gold around here. That could cause an avalanche of gold prospectors disrupting our lives and might bring disaster to the Maidu and us.'

Sean turned back to the boys.

'Lohat, I see you chose the leather shoes. That is a good choice, but for this country your moccasins are better. You will need to break in the white-man shoes before they will be comfortable.'

Lohat studied Sean for several moments.

'What means break in. I must break and ruin these shoes? No, I want to wear shoes.'

'No, no,' said Sean. 'You must wear these shoes for seven suns before you will enjoy wearing them. During that time, you feet may get sore and you may get blisters.'

He looked at Sean dumbly.

'What is blisters?'

Sean and Jennifer laughed, and Jennifer addressed the boys.

'You may get large sore spots on your heels after wearing the shoes for a few days. Tell your mother to treat the sore spots with her special medicinal herbs or come and see me or the Fruit Chief. I used to be a nurse in a white man's hospital and know how to treat blisters.'

Lohat shrugged and walked back to the group looking at his new shoes with happiness and a bit of concern.

Sean waited till they settled down and each boy had what he wanted out of the basket. He looked at the eight boys.

'Is that it? Is that all you want for these yellow stones? You can have more if you want it. I had no idea you would bring me so many of the yellow stones.'

The boys looked from one to the other and one boy stepped to the basket and picked up a knife, then stepped back with the others.

For some reason, the boys did not seem happy. Have I done something wrong? Sean wondered. Should I have discussed this trade with the Maidu fathers more carefully?

The group shuffled from foot to foot and glanced at one another. Finally, Ruma spoke.

'We are pleased with gifts, Fruit Chief, but we thought you would have one more gift for us, the thing we like most.'

Sean looked surprised. What could I possibly have missed? He wondered.

'Ruma, what is the one more thing you like most? Ask and I will give it to you if I can.'

Ruma glanced around at the other boys, who nodded and pointed toward Sean.

'The Toffee Candy!' said Ruma.

Sean and Jennifer laughed loudly and she ran into the house. When she returned she had one large bag of toffee and a smaller bag of hard candy. The boys eagerly took a handful of toffee and a handful of the hard candy, put it in their skin bags, and left the gold nuggets on the porch.

Sean smiled and glanced around at the boys.

'Is that it then? Are you satisfied with this trade?'

The boys looked at Ruma and coaxed him to speak.

'Could we bring you more yellow stones later? We have more.'

Sean didn't know what to say. He was in a state of shock.

Jennifer took Sean's arm. 'Sean, don't you dare take any more of those nuggets before you talk to the Maidu Chief about them. I want no discord with these friendly Indians.'

'Yes, I agree, Jenn, but whatever they bring, I will make it a point to talk it over with Chief Sam to be certain.'

Giving it one more try, Sean asked the boys, 'Are you sure your mother and father agree to this trade?'

The boys nodded and smiled big toothy grins.

In moments the boys had mounted their ponies and trotted off toward home, talking and yelling and showing off their new wealth to each other.

Sean sat on the porch, smoked his pipe, and looked in disbelief at the pile of gold.

'Well, I never!' said Jennifer as she sat down next to Sean, picked up several gold nuggets, and watched the boys ride away.

Sean laughed and shook his head.

'Doesn't look like much, does it? Such a small pile of nuggets, but when you weigh it and figure how much it's worth per ounce, the pile seems to get big, doesn't it, Jenn?'

She sat staring at the little mound on the porch and shaking her head as she dropped the nuggets in her hand into the pile.

'This is really interesting, Jenn. Those boys have worked through the harvest for over three weeks, and *we* ended up with fifty-three hundred dollars in gold. What a world!'

Sean glanced at her and shrugged. He wondered what more he could say to put her mind at rest.

He knew that to appease his wife, he would have to talk to Chief Sam again and maybe give the gold back. This gold exchange was in the hands of Chief Sam. Whatever the Chief decided, Sean would abide by his decision. After all, he thought, he didn't need the gold…did he?

Chapter 9

September 1847

A week later as Sean was picking up the remnants of the fruit and broken limbs in the plum orchard next to the house, he heard the Indian boys coming down the trail toward the orchards. Jennifer heard them and walked out on the porch wiping her hands. She shook her head.

'Sean, what did Chief Sam say about the nuggets the boys gave us?'

'He said they were pleased that we liked the yellow stones. The boys were happy and the mothers were making them new skin bags to hold more if they find them.'

'Don't they realize what these nuggets are worth?'

'Jenn, as I explained yesterday; gold is not a thing of value in their culture. I know that's hard to believe, but it's true. These Indians keep away from the white man's way of life. They are never seen in the general store in Chico according to Jon Simms. They are happy hunting, fishing, and living a simple life that agrees with them.

'Hannah Ehrens means well trying to teach them English and showing them how to grow their own food, but she's bucking an age-old way of life and doesn't realize the damage she may do to their culture.

'And we're the lucky recipients, Jenn.

'My main concern is that somehow the word will get out and our area will be overrun with prospectors looking for the mother lode. If there's gold around here, then there's gold all through the Sierra Nevada. And one day this area could be crowded with men looking for that wealth. Somehow I have to impress on the Maidu Indians that they must tell no one else about this gold. And for the time being, if Hannah doesn't know about the gold, then let's leave it that way. I for one do not intend to use this gold unless we absolutely have to. And if these orchards continue to improve in their output, we may *never* need the gold.'

Jennifer took his hands.

'Sean, you have provided us with a wonderful home and orchards. I can't believe we've been so fortunate. I agree with you. We don't need gold.' She looked across the orchards. 'Why, there's our gold...these orchards and the fruit of our labors. This must be what God meant for us. These *orchards* of gold.'

The boys approached the front porch and slid from their horses. Each held an animal skin pouch half-full of...gold nuggets? Sean wondered. Was that possible?

The boys placed their bags on the porch in a row, stood back, and watched Sean eagerly. Sean started to pick up a bag, hesitated, and then turned to Jennifer.

'Jenn, bring a table cloth, and you pick up this bag, will you? These look more full than the other bags they brought.'

She looked at him with interest, retrieved a table cloth which she spread on the porch, walked to the bag, reached down, and lifted it with surprise.

'You must be joking, Sean. This can't be full of gold nuggets.'

She handed the bag to Sean, straining slightly with the weight of the bag.

'Why, this may be heavier than the bags they gave us yesterday.'

He placed the bag on the porch and opened the pouch. Sure enough the bag was half-full of gold nuggets, some larger than the ones he had seen yesterday.

He walked to the shed with the boys following, and brought out the fruit balance scale. Ipsa held out his hand and Sean handed the scale to him. The boys smiled to each other as they watched Ipsa strain to carry the scale to the porch.

Sean placed the contents of the bag in the scale bowl and weighed it with lead weights.

The weight was exactly three pounds.

'Jenn, at twenty dollars an ounce, this bag contains almost one thousand dollars worth of gold! I can't believe it.'

He and Jennifer scanned the other seven bags, each one seeming to be about the same size and volume as the first.

'Why, there must be – eight thousand dollars worth of gold here plus the fifty-three-hundred dollars worth from yesterday; that's over thirteen thousand dollars worth of gold, Jenn. If this continues, we could almost pay off our mortgage on the property.'

Jennifer shook her head and pointed at Sean.

"Sean Kerry, you go talk to the Maidu Indians right this minute. I don't think they realize what they are giving you. They could be using this gold to make life easier for themselves. Maybe we should give it all back.'

Sean scratched his chin and looked at the bulging pouches.

'Jenn, I've had this discussion with the Maidu twice now, and the truth is they're simply not interested in this gold except as trinkets and jewelry for their wives. They realize it may be important to a white man like me, but they're happy with their lives and don't want to change their lifestyle and become like greedy white men who have treated them poorly in the past.

'It's the way we feel about their pottery and baskets. They're nice, but I wouldn't give you much for them. See the comparison, Jenn?

'I know how you feel. And I feel the same…greedy, and guilty for taking this gold from them like this, but think about it for a minute. If they take this gold to Chico, word will get out and this whole area will be crawling with prospectors in no time. You know what happens when greed gets loose with white men. They'll steal us blind and the Indians, too, and worse. The kind of riff-raff that will show up is not pleasant to think on. I say we should put this gold in a safe hiding place until we need it – which may be never – and forget about it for now. Maybe we can do something nice for the Maidu later with some of the gold, but not right now. If we were to use any of it ourselves, we'd open the door to just what I mentioned. It would change our lives forever. We might even have to move again.

'You know, Jenn, I spent several weeks researching the finding of gold, and in every case where gold was found disastrous results followed every time all the way back to the 1500's. Ms. Calm at the Chico Library helped me with the research, and she ordered several books from other libraries for me. Just show a white man one gold nugget and there will be prospectors all over the area overnight. We don't want that, and I warned the Indians about showing gold to white men, too.

As happened yesterday, the boys chose from the wicker basket Jennifer placed on the porch, and were finally ready to go home with more simple treasures, this time cloth shirts, pants, and belts plus more knives and hatchets.

Sean watched the lame boy, Ipsa, as he hobbled around with the other boys in the orchard. He thought of Doctor Bryant who he had met in Chico and wondered if the doctor could do something for the boy's leg. He would talk to Bryant about it on his next trip.

When the trading was over, the boys gathered their possessions and walked their ponies out to the orchards where they went to work cleaning up the debris left from the harvest. In a few hours they rode home.

On his next trip to the Maidu village, Sean talked to Chief Sam about the gold. The old Chief smiled.

'The yellow stones are our secret, yours and mine. We no tell, you no tell. They are worthless unless we tell other white men, right? You keep stones. Some day you may need.'

And that was it. Sean could see that the Chief understood about the value of the nuggets, but as long as they both kept this secret, no harm would come to the Maidu or Sean due to the gold. He liked that plan, for in effect, he was saving for a rainy day.

Sean then approached Ipsa's father, and in his halting use of their language, suggested that Sean take the boy to the Chico doctor to see if anything could be done for his leg. At first the boy's father was reluctant, but finally agreed.

'I trust you, Fruit Chief. Maybe white medicine man can help my son. I would like to see him run and play with the other boys like he did before the horse fell on him.'

Later when in Chico delivering fruit, Sean stopped in and talked with Doc Bryant about Ipsa's leg.

'Bring him in, Sean, and we'll see what can be done for him. But don't give his folks any hope till I see what's what.'

Sean agreed and made arrangements for Ipsa to see the doctor.

A few days later as they rode to Chico in Sean's wagon, Ipsa looked frightened, knowing he would soon see the white medicine man, but once he met Doc Bryant and found that he spoke his language, he relaxed while the doctor examined him.

'From what I can feel, it's a compound fracture. The weight of that horse broke the femur and moved the bone ends apart. Also, the tibia has sustained damage, but I won't know how extensive it is till I open his leg. I'm surprised that the boy is able to get around at all the way his leg is. I'd say all in all, I could have him running again in fifteen to twenty weeks if all goes well, although he may have a slight limp.

They agreed on a day for Sean to bring the boy in for the surgery, and on the way back to the Maidu village, Sean explained what the doctor said in much simpler terms.

On the day of the surgery, Ipsa was nervous and asked Sean to stay with him until the cutting was finished, and Sean agreed. Dr. Bryant looked at his two bottles of anesthetic: Ether and Chloroform. His main problem in the past had been to obtain an adequate supply of both since the manufacturing process had just been refined. Both had about the same effect on patients and had now been used successfully since about 1840. He finally chose ether.

In two hours the job was completed, and Ipsa's leg was put in a cast. He lay groggy from the anesthesia, and complained of the bad taste in his mouth. He got sick once and threw up, but was soon sitting up and drinking milk from a large glass.

His face showed disappointment, thinking this was the way his leg would be from now on, but Sean explained that the cast would be on for one or two moons till the bones healed.

'Once the cast is removed,' said Sean, 'you must exercise your leg as the doctor prescribes, and in no time, you should be able to run and jump again.

* * *

On a day twenty-two weeks later, as Sean made his normal fruit delivery to the Maidu village, he watched the boys at play and saw Ipsa running and dodging with the rest. As he turned his wagon around for the return trip to home, Ipsa ran up and grabbed Sean's arm.

'Thank you, Fruit Chief, for giving me new leg. Someday I show you where we find yellow stones, but first I talk to Ruma.'

Sean smiled and roughed the boy's short hair.

'I am happy that your leg is better, Ipsa. Doctor Bryant is a fine medicine man and used much of his magic to heal you. I will see you and the other boys soon, for I have another harvest coming up.'

And with that he waved to Oakum who was repairing one of the Indian huts, turned for home, lit his pipe, and soon after, found he was whistling a happy tune.

Chapter 10

September 1847

At the end of September, Sean's son, Finn Kerry rode in from Chico on a rented horse from the Person Livery Stables. Sean and Jennifer were caught by surprise. They both hugged him and showed him his room which overlooked the Kerry Orchards as their master bedroom did.

'What a place,' said Finn enthusiastically as he glanced around. 'I had no idea the house was so beautiful. Mom, you have to take me through it and show me everything. I can see this home has quality written all over it.'

Sean eyed him with curiosity.

'Well, Finn, are you ready to help me in our new orchards, or do you still have more work to do on your book?'

Finn threw up his hands and said, 'I'm free as a bird, Dad. My book is in the hands of Hanford Publishing now, for better or worse.'

'You never did tell me the title, son. What is it? You can tell us now that it's finished.'

'I was afraid to tell you till I had the book completed and sold, Dad. I knew if you read it, I'd probably get a lot of static from you or suggestions for changes. I wanted to avoid all that.'

'Okay, so what's the title?'

Finn smiled at them both.

'*The Orchardist's Dream.*"

'How wonderful, Finn,' said Jennifer. 'What a nice title.'

'So I assume it's about growing things, right?' asked Sean.

Finn laughed.

'You bet, Dad. I took everything you taught me and put it in a book–with a few additions here and there, of course. I have a copy upstairs for you. Hope you like it.

'So, let me change my clothes and you can show me the orchards. I can't wait to see them.'

For over a month after Finn Kerry arrived at the new Kerry Orchards, he worked with Sean and the boys in the orchards and learned the Indian language more rapidly than Sean had. With his first novel, *The Orchardist's Dream,* being prepared for publication, Finn had high hopes for the marketing of his book.

The Maidu Indians were intrigued by how much Finn looked like his father.

Finn worked in the apricot orchard on the day that Hannah Ehrens rode up on her big chestnut and sat watching him. Finally, she rode her horse close to the tree where he was working.

'Hello. You must be Finn Kerry. At first I thought you were Sean.'

Finn looked down at her, saw this lovely blonde apparition in front of him, and almost lost his balance on the ladder. Embarrassed, he climbed down awkwardly and stood looking at this beautiful tanned girl with the long blonde hair. She was the vision of a girl Finn had always dreamed of meeting.

'Yes, I'm Finn Kerry. And you are…?'

She laughed, for she could see that he was flustered by her arrival.

'Hannah. Hannah Ehrens. Sean told me about you and your publishing career. He said you were writing a novel. How exciting. I don't think I could ever do that.'

Finn put his shoulder bag half-full of apricots on the ground, but the strap slipped from his wet hands, and the apricots tumbled out on the damp ground.

Hannah slipped from her horse and bent down next to Finn while he picked up the spilled fruit.

'Here, let me help you. I'm sorry; I guess I surprised you by sneaking up that way.'

While they picked up the apricots, their shoulders brushed together once or twice, and Finn felt something like a thin electric shock that made his knees feel weak and his pulse race.

'So, what are you doing here, Hannah?'

'Oh, I come over when I can and help your dad with the orchards. He's teaching me all about growing fruit and I just love working with the plants. Don't you?'

'Yes, I do...my dad taught me all I know about growing fruits. He made a convert out of me years ago, but I have always been partial to words, too, so I tried to make a career in the publishing business. That's when I met Gerald Mann, the Senior Editor at Hanford Publishing, and he changed my life–well, at least for a little while. He liked my work and convinced me to write a novel. It's been an experience with the research and hours of writing and rewriting. But now that my novel is finished, I realized that I missed the orchards a lot, and so – here I am, too.'

'What's the title of your novel, Finn?'

'*The Orchardist's Dream,*' he said.

'Hmm, I bet that gets a lot of attention. I can see you're much taken with growing things. Even the title of your book shows it. I'd sure like to read it sometime.'

Finn found himself nodding at everything she said. He tried to imagine the life of an orchardist with a beautiful woman like Hannah to help him.

She smiled at him and studied him closely.

'You certainly do look like your father. Why you could almost be brothers.'

They talked on and finally adjourned to the house with Hannah riding her chestnut mare next to Finn as he walked with the bag of apricots over his shoulder. They had lunch with his mother and the three of them sat on the porch with lemonade while they waited for Sean to appear.

After a while Hannah had to leave, said goodbye, and rode off toward Chico.

Finn watched her ride away and kept watching until she was out of sight.

'Finn? Are you all right?' asked Jennifer. Then she looked at him with that knowing look and nodded. 'Lordy, I think you're smitten, Finn Kerry.'

She laughed and gave him a hug, and, embarrassed, he hugged her back.

'She's beautiful, isn't she, mom?'

Jennifer giggled and clipped him on the shoulder.

* * *

Almost from the first day Hannah visited the Kerry orchards, hoping to learn more about growing fine fruits like Sean's, Finn was ready and eager to teach this exciting girl. Finn was immediately attracted to Hannah, and before long they attended local dances in Chico, rode on trips of exploration around the Sacramento River and Deer Creek, and delved into each other's histories, lives, and aspirations for the future, but Hannah still had feelings toward Sean.

A few days later when Finn and his mother had gone to Chico to deliver fruit and do some shopping, Hannah worked with Sean in the plum orchard.

'By the way, Sean, at the beginning when I first showed the young Maidu Indians how to plant corn, most of the plowing and planting of the corn was done by the Indian boys. Would have been nice if we were in the corn-planting season, but we'll just have to wait till next May. In early August I had the Maidu planting peas, carrots, beets, spinach, and lettuce from seed, and now they are seeing the vegetables maturing. This will give them some food for the winter months since these will continue growing in this climate right into December.'

'That's wonderful, Hannah. Your program has really paid off. I can see in the boys that growing food is now more than just an idea. They have now planted corn, and they have vegetables, too. Is that progress or what?'

Needing to replace a piece of clay irrigation pipe that Oakum had broken, Sean and Hannah walked to his shed. While he cut a piece of the clay pipe to size, Hannah explored the shed, saw the wall full of interesting tools, and noticed the horse stable where Sean's horse stood chewing fresh hay. She noticed the hay loft attached over the stable, and as she stood with her hand on the stable ladder, Sean noticed her look up.

'It's a small hayloft, Hannah. Climb up and take a look if you're a mind to.'

She climbed seductively, posing several times suggestively while she looked down at Sean. Sean watched her, and suddenly filled with desire, followed her up the ladder. When he reached the top, Hannah stood facing him, almost against him, and he nearly fell backward, but she grabbed his arm, pulled him close, and kissed him before he could resist. But his resistance didn't last long.

'Hannah, I...'

She kissed him again, his desire took over, and he embraced her as they fell into the loose hay behind her. Without another thought, Hannah began to undress, and in the heat of the moment, Sean followed suit and made love to her. After lying with Hannah for half an hour, Sean rose to his feet and shook his head at her resolutely as he quickly put on his pants and shirt.

'Hannah, I'm ashamed that I let this happen. You took me by surprise, although, I admit, I have wanted you every time I see you, but I'm a married man, and I feel I took advantage of you. I'm sorry.'

'No, no, Sean. I've yearned for you almost from the first time I saw you in the Maidu village. I know what a good man you are. If we can't have a full life together, I will have to be content to meet you like this...'

'No! This can't happen again, Hannah. Please, understand. If I were a free man, I would jump at the chance to be with you, to woo you, and even take you to wife, but I'm happily married for twenty-four years, and that's all there is to it. We can't meet like this again. Please try to understand. My wife is here now, and I could never feel right about this again. In fact, I'm feeling terribly guilty right this minute.'

She gave him a sad look, dressed in a slow and provocative way while she watched him covertly, and climbed down the ladder behind him. They never mentioned the episode again.

Four weeks later, Hannah became concerned. She had missed her regular period and that was important since she was always prompt. Then one morning she was nauseated upon rising, and her breasts felt tender and seemed to be fuller.

She also noticed that she was more tired than usual in the afternoons, and short trips left her exhausted. She knew her own body well, and knew that she was one of the healthiest women around. She wondered if she was imagining things.

Suddenly she sat up with her eyes wide. She became frightened as a possibility crossed her mind.

Was she pregnant? She wondered. She had no experience in that direction. Oh Lord, it's been a month or more since her and Sean…

She contemplated the consequences of a pregnancy. Having a baby as an unmarried woman in the Chico society was simply not done. Her reputation would be ruined, her father would be shunned by the community, and no man would ever look at her as a potential wife again, at least not in Chico, California.

Did this mean that she had to leave home? Where would she go, how would she support herself – and a baby? If she was pregnant her baby needed a father, and she knew she could not tell Sean or her father. What could they possibly do for her?

Then she thought of Finn Kerry. She felt certain that Finn would marry her. She was sure he loved her, and surprisingly as she thought about it, she loved him, too.

Her mind whirled with strange thoughts. The timing might be about right if she could get Finn to propose right away, she thought. If they married quickly, no one would ever know. She considered this more and finally devised a plan of action. She would have to be as bold as she had been with Sean. This would work, she knew it would. It had to work, she decided. And besides, she *did* love Finn. She was not being devious. Eventually even without a push, Finn would marry her. This would only speed things up a bit.

Chapter 11

October 1847

Three days later when she saw Finn in town, she asked him to meet her at the Maidu village the next morning, and he agreed.

Although she still had strong feelings for happily married Sean Kerry, her pregnancy changed everything. She could not even go to Sean or her father for help.

She was waiting near Chief Sam's hut when Finn rode into the village the next day.

'Hi, Finn. Come, I want to show you something.'

Finn dismounted, tied his horse to a post, and followed her as she led him to the outskirts of the village to an unusually well-made tepee painted with birds and plants and flowers all over the light animal skin coverings.

She took his hand and led him into the small lodge.

'Forgive me, Finn, but I asked Chief Sam if we could use this special place for our meeting.'

He looked around him. The floor of the room was filled with two and three layers of soft-looking furs. Lamps hung from several poles. Flowers had been placed at various spots in the room and he could imagine that they were in their own secret garden. On a small table were two glasses filled with a colored liquid, and beside it was a bowl of fruit. In the center of the room a small fire burned with practically no smoke. He watched the fine tendrils of smoke rise straight up and out the center hole at the top.

'As I said, this is a special room to the Maidu. It is often used for newly paired couples when they decide to share their lives, and I thought maybe we should come here to talk and see whether we might be one of those couples.

Finn looked at her in surprise, for he had been thinking of asking her to marry him for weeks, but until his book was published, he had no real income except what money Sean paid him for his work in the orchards.

Finn could smell the fragrant perfume that Hannah wore, and he noticed a flower in her blonde hair, something he had never seen before. Her skirt and blouse were of some delicate material, and it seemed to him that he could see right through them in the dim light.

He stepped closer to her and she took his hands and led him onto the thick furs.

'You do love me, don't you, Finn?' She asked as she drew him closer.

He looked into her blue eyes and saw magic there as she folded her arms about his neck. Without thinking, he kissed her and she responded. His hands began to explore her and she drew closer to him, and he suddenly found himself rolling on the soft furs with Hannah clinging to him.

'Oh Finn, I've wanted you for so long...'

'Hannah, I'm so in love with you.'

They embraced again and soon they were out of their cumbersome clothes and making love.

Later, Finn held her close and she clung to him eagerly.

'Hannah, would you...that is, could you ever marry an orchardist like me? I don't have a big income at the moment, but I know fruit growing, and we could start our own orchard. Maybe Dad would give us some acreage to start. What do you think?'

She murmured softly and kissed him on the ear, the cheek, the nose, and his mouth, a soft kiss that he wished would last forever.

'Oh Finn, I thought you would never ask me. You must know I love you. I can hardly wait to be your wife. Let's not wait. Let's tell your parents and get married right away. Can we, darling Finn?'

'I'll tell my father tomorrow while we're out in the orchard working. I know he'll be surprised.'

She looked away as he said this.

The next morning when he awoke, Finn stared at the roof of the teepee and tried to remember his dreams. They were about him and Hannah. He looked over at her sleeping form, her blonde hair spread out seductively around her. This is the woman who is to be my wife, he thought with amazement. He bent over and kissed her forehead gently, and then rose and walked to the teepee flaps. Outside the sun was rising, and Finn could see it would be a beautiful day. He took a deep breath, threw up his arms and yelled, 'Yes!', and a passing Indian woman glanced at him, smiled, and continued on her way with a final glance back at him, still smiling.

Finn and Hannah parted that morning, and each took their happy news back to their parents.

Finn worked in the orchards the next day, picking fruit while standing on a ladder, waiting for his father to appear. He was humming and singing and the Indian boys were watching him. As Sean entered the orchard, he heard Finn singing and stopped to watch him.

'You sound awful cheerful today, Finn. Never heard you sing like this before. Is something going on that I should know about?'

'You bet I'm cheerful, Dad. Last night was a life-changing event for me.'

'Really? Life-changing? What happened?'

'Dad, I proposed to Hannah and she accepted.'

Sean stared at him and didn't know what to say.

'Hmm, my goodness. Congratulations, Finn. That's wonderful news. You couldn't have found a better woman. I guess there's a wedding in your future,' he said with a big smile.

'Yes, we plan to have the wedding before the end of the month. That's what Hannah wants. We'd like to have it here, Dad, if that's okay with you. It'll be a small wedding with just a few friends; Pat Ehrens, Chief Sam, and the Indian boys and their parents.'

At Hannah's urging, their wedding was arranged within a week. A small group of people attended the wedding at the Kerry Orchards: Sean and Jennifer Kerry, Pat Ehrens who gave away the bride, the eight Indian boys and their parents, Chief Sam and the Methodist minister from Chico.

* * *

As the final question was asked of Hannah, she said, 'I do', and kissed Finn boldly in front of the group of well-wishers as the minister finished pronouncing them man and wife. The wedding over, everyone danced to fiddle music and Sean played his flute for the first time in ages. As happened before, the Indian boys were enthralled by Sean's playing and when he finished, they wanted to see his magical flute again, so Sean passed it among the boys and everyone had an enjoyable evening.

Hannah and Finn prepared to leave, and everyone threw rice and wished them well as they rode off in the wagon toward the Sacramento River for their honeymoon.

Within a week they were back at the orchards working together as man and wife, just as Finn had envisioned. They lived in one wing of the large Kerry house and love triumphed. Sean snickered to Jennifer as they watched Finn walk around in a daze.

'Now there is a happily married man, Jenn. I know just how he feels,' he said as he pulled her to him and kissed her.

They were married a month when Hannah announced at dinner that she was pregnant, and the evening turned into a family celebration.

That night as they prepared for bed, Finn embraced Hannah and kissed her tenderly.

'Ah Hannah, you have made me a happy man. Our first child will be a boy, and we will name him after my grandfather, Ryan Kerry. Is that all right with you?'

She embraced him tightly, and kissed him gently on both cheeks.

'Whatever you want, Finn. And he will be the first of many.'

'Good! That's the way I see it, too, Hannah. We'll fill the Kerry house with children. And who knows, maybe we won't need the Maidu Indian boys to help us in the orchards in a few years.'

She laughed and said, 'whatever you say, Finn.'

Chapter 12

October 1847

The pale orange sun rose slowly in the misty east as Sean gathered the eight boys around him under the apple tree. Finn sat in the rear listening to his father along with the boys.

'Since our apple harvest is over, it is time to be thinking about pears. Pears are a delicious fruit that can grow in a wide range of soils. Here I have a perfect soil with a small percentage of loam, and a mixture of clay that gives the root system stability. As you can see the trees are planted about twenty-five feet apart. I use the drip irrigation system on the pears like I do on our other fruit trees.

'I fertilize with 2 ounces of ammonium nitrate for each year of growth. I try to get about one foot of height each season by controlling the amount of fertilizer used. As the tree grows from a central leader, I must train the branches so that they don't interfere with each other; this allows the fruit to have room to grow better. Sometimes I use a spreader like this to shape the branches and let them spread outward. It has 'V-shaped' ends so it can be attached to two branches as I see fit.

'We will harvest the pears when they are still hard and let them ripen at room temperature. If you remember, I keep the picked pears in containers in that cool dark cellar on the side of the house. That way I can keep the pears for up to two months before taking them to Chico or giving them to your tribe.

'Now let's talk a bit about pruning. I mentioned this to you with the apples, and most of our fruits are pruned in the same general way. I choose to prune my trees in December and January which is Omhuncholi and Yegoni in your language.'

The boys glanced at each other and laughed at Sean's pronunciations.

'Cuts close to the central trunk heal faster. We can prune part or all of a branch. We want the tree shaped almost like the shape of the fruit, usually with full bottoms and thinning toward a point or crown at the top. With apples we want to have an open center so that fruit gets plenty of sunlight, but with pears most of the fruit grows toward the outside and we prune so that the outer shape sees lots of sun during the day. I usually prune all the trees when the leaves fall off so that I can see what I'm doing better. With young trees I prune them heavily for better growth. As you will see with the pear trees, I do most of my pruning in the top of the tree, and I use this technique for all of our fruit trees; apples, apricots, plums, and pears. With these four varieties, I try to prune or remove about twenty percent of last year's growth.

'Here are my three preferred tools for pruning: this hand shear, a lopping shear with long handles which is great for the thicker branches since they give you much greater leverage, and finally the pruning saw which is small and makes it easy to saw off limbs almost anywhere on the tree.

'I have enough tools for each of you, so let's try this on a few trees so I can show you how I would do it, and you can ask questions.'

They worked through the morning, the boys taking their cues from Sean and Finn as they pruned the trees in one row, and finally Sean called a break for lunch. Each boy had brought his own lunch fixed by his mother, and Sean added dessert made by Jennifer. They gathered under a huge oak tree with plenty of shade, good branches one could climb into to eat, and a small stream nearby for water. Finn walked to the house to have lunch with Hannah and his mother. Finn and Hannah soon left in the wagon, headed for Chico to do some shopping.

Throughout the afternoon the boys worked on the trees and by the late afternoon, Sean called them together and they cleaned and put away their tools. Then together they walked among the trees to see how well the pruning had gone. Sean made several minor suggestions, but in general, felt well-pleased with the work they had done. When the boys looked ready to leave, Ruma approached Sean.

'Fruit Chief, you have been good to the Maidu. Our fathers like you for your kindness and honesty, and for all the fruits you give to our people.

'We have decided to show you our source of the yellow stones you treasure so much. You will be the only white man to know. You must promise never to tell another white man about this. If you agree, we will ride with you to this magical place in the morning before we start to prune more trees.'

Sean could hardly contain his enthusiasm.

'Well, Ruma. You have me curious. I look forward to our trip tomorrow. How long will we be gone? Is there anything I need to bring?'

Ruma thought for a moment.

'Bring water skin in case you get thirsty and good hat with wide brim to guard against hot sun. Your old horse can make this trip easy. We should be back in three hours or less.'

And with that the boys hopped on their ponies and rode for home.

* * *

Early the next morning, the boys gathered at Sean's porch and Jennifer talked to them as Sean saddled his horse. Finn and Hannah were still asleep. When Sean was ready he rode to the porch and Jennifer handed him a bag of snacks for the boys and a water skin which he hung on his saddle horn.

The boys set off to the northeast, winding through the brushy countryside as they headed toward the foothills of the Sierra Nevada Mountains. Soon they were in rocky territory, with scattered clumps of pine trees, large boulders, and walls of stone which increased in height as they ascended. Occasionally they had to walk their horses due to the loose rock. The trees disappeared and the trail became rocky and dusty with few plants and small bushes. Sean saw a large lizard sitting on a rock. The sun was already hot and Sean, glad he had brought the wide-brimmed hat, pulled the brim down over his forehead. They climbed a steep animal trail, and before long, Sean looked up at the towering rock walls in front of them. This may be some kind of butte or mesa, he thought, but he couldn't tell from so close. They followed the animal trail along the face of the rock wall, dodging the large and small rocks that cluttered the base of the wall, and finally stopped at a small cluster of pine trees, the first trees Sean had seen at this elevation.

'Are we getting close?' asked Sean.

The boys chuckled and pointed at the trees. They slid off their ponies, let them roam freely. Sean tied Martin to a small bush and followed through the trees behind the boys.

Beyond the trees Sean saw only the solid rock face before him, and suddenly realized that the boys were disappearing from view. And then he watched as Ruma motioned to him and disappeared into a slight crevice in the wall. Sean followed, edging sideways around a pine tree growing at the narrow cleft which effectively hid the opening. The fissure continued for a while but hardly wavered in its width. He glanced upward and saw nothing but smooth rock on both sides of him. Sean realized that he was looking at an ancient shift in the solid rock. Ahead Sean heard a roar which continued as he walked.

Suddenly above the roar, one of the Indian boys yelled, and Sean stepped out of the split in the wall into a one-hundred-foot-diameter cylindrical space completely surrounded by rock walls. In the center of the space was a dark pool surrounded by large rocks, and flowing into the pool was a waterfall falling from at least two-hundred feet above.

Sean walked to the edge of the pool which seemed to be dark yet clear water, but he couldn't tell how deep since the falling water kept the surface wavy with scattered water on the surface, and the falling water gave off a swirl of mist. In moments they were all soaked from the mists around the falling water.

The boys had gathered near the rocks beside the fall. Ipsa walked to Sean.

'I will show you how we get yellow stones, Fruit Chief.' And with that he dove off a rock ledge into the center of the pool. He was gone for some time and suddenly popped to the surface with one hand in a fist. He swam to shore, stood before Sean, and opened his clenched fist. In the palm of his hand lay a beautiful gold nugget about one inch in diameter. Sean took it, turned it over and over and said, 'Wow! That's the biggest nugget I've seen. You mean there are more like that?'

They boys laughed.

'There are many stones like this one in the bottom of the magic pool—too many to count. We do not know how they came to be here, but this pool is full of them,' said Ruma.

'How deep is the pool, Ruma?' asked Sean.

Ruma thought for a moment.

'Bottom is – three tall hunters from surface.'

Sean did some quick figuring. A Maidu hunter was generally about five-and-a-half-to six-feet tall. So the bottom was about sixteen to eighteen feet deep—as deep as he'd ever dived. He knew he would feel the pressure in his ears if he tried to dive to the bottom.

Sean took off his hat, shirt, pants, and shoes and stepped up on the rock ledge. The boys yelled encouragement. He made a clean dive into the center and the falling water forced him to the bottom quickly. He felt his ears pop. He opened his eyes, but the dim light wavered, and he could not see much, but he had the impression that the bottom was filled with small stones or gravel. He scooped up a few pebbles off the bottom and pushed off for the surface. When he broke the surface the boys cheered and gathered around him as he stood on the shore. Sean worked his jaws and tried to clear the water from his ears.

He opened his hand and found three pebbles; one was only stone, but the other two were small gold nuggets.

He realized that since they had arrived they had uncovered about eight ounces of gold – about one hundred, sixty dollars worth. And in less than two minutes, he thought. He laughed to himself as he imagined the usual method of panning for gold which netted a prospector a few tenths of an ounce or less for each swirling pan full of gravel. He definitely liked this method better.

'Have you seen enough, Fruit Chief?' asked Ruma.

Sean nodded his head as he looked all around the pool area, the sound of the waterfall pounding in his ears.

'Let me sit a minute and study this waterfall,' he said.

He knew that at the top there must be a large stream flowing over rocks to make the waterfall. Also, the size of the waterfall would depend on the size of a rain. Theorizing, Sean figured that during a large rain, the size of the nuggets flowing over the natural dam at the top would be larger, and in near-drought conditions–if the stream still flowed–the nuggets would be small, maybe the size of a grain of sand.

He shaded his eyes and looked up at the top of the waterfall. He wondered how deep the water behind the natural dam at the top could be. If deep, then the chances of large nuggets below that dam could be great. It would be worth investigating.

'Ruma, is there a way to get to the top of the waterfall?'

'Yes, Fruit Chief. I knew you would ask. There are many steps and handholds in the rock face, steps that have been here for much past time, maybe thousands of years. As you would say, they are ancient.'

'Have you been to the top?'

'Only once. It is a hard climb, and since it is so easy to find yellow stones in the magic pool, climbing the rock face is not worth the effort.'

'How long would it take us to climb to the top and come back down?'

Ruma thought about it.

'One-half hour up and one-half hour down maybe.'

'Okay. I think I've seen enough for now. Would you mind if I came here by myself?'

'No mind. Father knew you might want to. He only asked that you keep this magic pool secret from other white men.'

'I agree. In fact, tell Chief Sam that I do not intend to tell anyone or show anyone the gold, and have decided I will not use it unless I am forced to because my orchards fail.'

'If greedy white men knew about gold in a place like this, your village and my home and orchards would be overrun with prospectors searching for gold. They would destroy this waterfall and all the surrounding lands. The waters would be ruined in a short time, and nothing would grow near here. That is the gift white men leave behind wanting to be rich.

'Yes, you say what my father, the Chief, say. Let us go back to your orchards. It is time to prune.'

Sean laughed.

The ride back was silent as Sean thought about what the Maidu had shown him. He knew that he was now deeply in debt to this gentle people, and knew that their 'magic pool' must be kept secret forever. He wasn't certain he should even tell Jennifer about this, although it would be difficult to keep a secret from his wife.

Chapter 13

October 1847

A week later with no immediate harvest due for a while, a day the boys had gone hunting with their fathers and uncles, Sean decided he would visit the 'magic pool', and climb to the top of the waterfall. Taking a large coil of thin rope with him on his horse, several empty cornmeal bags, and a water bag, he made the trip to the opening quicker than he thought, and within half an hour he stood beside the deep dark pool.

He found the hand-holds Ruma had mentioned, and with his water skin around his neck, the rope coiled over his shoulder, and the bags tucked into his shirt, he climbed the wall. They were indeed centuries old steps, but deep enough to afford a solid grip. He had to brush the accumulated dust and dirt from some of the steps as he climbed. In about a half hour, Sean reached the top and rested while he watched the waters flow over the edges of the natural dam. He dropped the rope and bags on the rocky shore of the stream.

He looked up the stream which disappeared in the distance between huge rocks, and glanced into the water near the dam. Sean stepped into the water and stood for a moment to the side of the dam feeling the drag of the water on his legs. Surprisingly, the water was not too deep, maybe three or four feet in front of the dam, and the flow was not as fast as he expected. He felt certain that he was too large to be swept over the edge of the dam, so he slowly sank into the water and began exploring the bottom with his hands near the center of the dam.

In moments he scooped up handfuls of nuggets of every size, easily distinguished from rock by the smoothness of the gold; he sorted each handful before throwing them on the bank near his bags. Most were as large as or larger than the ones the boys had given him. This natural dam had gathered the larger nuggets for years, he thought.

He waded ashore and laid out the cornmeal bags. He sat down and began to stuff nuggets into the bags. In a few minutes, he realized that the bags would be too heavy for him to carry down the wall, so he stopped. He would have to think of some way to get these larger nuggets down to the pool. Probably the best way would be to tie the bags to the rope and lower the bags to the bottom. If only Finn were here, he thought.

He tied the three bags to the end of the rope, lowered them down with difficulty because of the total weight, tossed the top end of the rope over the side, and began the climb down. In less than a half hour, he reached the bottom and took a guess at the weight of his bags full of nuggets. He figured he had averaged about fifteen pounds of gold nuggets per bag on this first trip. He had about fifteen thousand dollars worth of gold—and there was so much more at the top and bottom of the waterfall. He was beginning to feel greedy. Three cornmeal bags of fifteen pounds each was a good amount. He decided he would try to make one trip per week to the waterfall alone and gather what he could. Next time, he thought, he would bring a small pick axe to loosen some of the larger chunks behind the dam. He was sure there were some nuggets over four or five pounds if he could dig them free. He knew that in about six weeks the next harvest would begin, so he would work toward one-hundred-thousand dollars worth of gold as his goal. He returned to his horse, tied the bags onto his saddle horn, and rode slowly for home.

This had been a good day's work, he thought with excitement.

He would have to think about a good place to hide all this gold, but as his mind thought of hiding spots, he was sure he knew just the place.

Soon Sean formed a weekly excursion to the 'golden' pool with the boys, and they would dive to the bottom and scoop up fistfuls of various sized nuggets and give them to Sean.

He had not told Jennifer or Finn about his hiding place, and knew that he must do that soon. He was not certain why he hesitated to tell them, but he attributed it to greed. He would tell them soon, maybe at dinner one night, and they would celebrate.

* * *

Finn looked out the kitchen window and saw a horse approaching. He walked to the porch and was surprised to see Gerald Mann, his old mentor. The visit by Gerald Mann from Hanford Publishing Company came as a surprise, and Finn felt flustered by the attention this great editor heaped upon him. Finn introduced Hannah to Mann, and the man was struck wordless by Finn's wife, an uncommon occurrence for Mann, thought Finn with an inner smile.

'I was in the neighborhood of Chico and thought this would be a good chance to see you again. The book committee loved your book, Finn, and with your book as the centerpiece, Hanford wants to do a campaign on 'planting, plants, orchards, and growing techniques to run for six months. So there's lots of preparation to be made.

'First, I'd like to give you this check, an advance on your book. Believe it or not I read your book twice, and was elated both times. Now comes the marketing, Finn, and with you as the spearhead, we have two other plant-type authors who will share the limelight with you. Hanford may – no, *will* – ask you to appear at selected bookstores, read passages to readers, and sign your book for buyers. Of course, all of your travel expenses will be paid.

'The other two authors are Charles Temple, Chuck for short, whose book is, '*Green Beginnings*' and Tyler McPherson whose book is *Grass Roots*'.

'Between the three of you, Hanford wants to sweep the country with the idea of readers doing their own thing in the garden and even having an orchard like yours. What do you think, Finn? Are you interested in being part of this group?'

Finn was nodding and felt like he had a million questions. But he settled for:

'Can I bring my wife on these trips, Gerald?'

Mann laughed and said, 'After seeing your wife, Finn, I don't believe Hanford would have it any other way. You have a beautiful wife, and she'll fit perfectly with the photographic spreads the company will want for newspaper and magazine ads.'

Finn invited Mann to dinner and to stay the night, and when Mann accepted, he asked, 'Um, are your wife and mother good cooks, Finn?'

Finn laughed and nodded.

The next morning, Mann left for Chico on his rented horse so he could take the stage coach for Reno. Finn was happy for days and went into the orchard singing, whistling, and humming for hours. Hannah was ecstatic about a trip to faraway cities, for she had never travelled in her life. And to be included in the advertisements for Finn's book was an even more pleasant surprise. Sean and Jennifer patted him on the back and wished him well with the impending trips he and Hannah would make for the sake of Finn's book.

* * *

Within two months, Finn and Hannah made three trips at Hanford Publishing's expense, signing books with the two other authors and posing for photographs for advertising publications.

Hannah was ecstatic with the wonderful stores in the three large cities, and shopped to her heart's content. Of the three cities; St. Louis, Chicago, and New York, Hannah was enthralled with New York the most. The restaurants were like nothing she had ever seen, and she and Finn took tours all around the city at every opportunity.

At the end of their whirlwind book tour, they were both tired and looking ready for home at the Kerry Orchards. They had seen their photographs in the important newspapers, had had an interview with a top magazine, and had been wined and dined by two of the top book publishers in New York.

Their trip home was partly by train, partly by stage coach, and finally by wagon furnished by Jon Simms in Chico, and as they stepped down from the wagon in front of their home, Jennifer, the children, and Big ran down the porch steps to welcome them home.

Over the next two years Finn received royalties promptly in every quarter, until the book began to lose ground to newer books coming out all the time.

Except for the wonderful book tour, Finn wondered whether all his hard work on the book was worth the effort. He realized that he was happy to be back at work in the orchards, working with the Maidu Indian boys again.

Chapter 14

November 1847

One day in November, 1847 when Sean was almost to the Maidu village on his horse, he heard a girl's screams and rode toward the source of the commotion. He found two white men wearing side arms attacking one of the Yamadi Maidu Indian girls. They had her on the ground and had ripped part of her rabbit-skin garment off. Having no guns, Sean tried to intervene by running down one of the men with his horse, but the other man turned and shot Sean, and he fell from his horse severely wounded, blood running down his face.

When the Indians heard the gunshot, they rushed to the spot, found the gunmen, and saw Sean lying on the ground with blood running from his head. The young girl screamed and ran toward the Indians, and the gunmen made for their horses when they saw the Indians, both sending random shots at the Maidu hunters as they rode off.

Immediately the Indians shot arrows at the fleeing men, and two arrows found their mark in the last man. He fell forward on his horse and yelled to his partner for help. The lead man grabbed the reins and led the horse into the trees where they disappeared before the Indians could target them again. Later as the Indians tracked the fleeing men, they found one of the men dead lying against a tree. His pockets had been turned out and his horse was gone. His friend, knowing he was dead, had robbed the body, took the horse, and disappeared.

The Maidu ran to Sean thinking he may be dead, but he was breathing, barely. They took him to their village and several of the women tended to his wound which was in the right side of his head. They saw that the ball had gone through the right side of his skull and exited in the rear. The path of the bullet didn't seem to have gone deeply into Sean's head.

One of the Maidu hunters grabbed an Indian pony, shouted to the others and spurred the horse in the direction of Chico in search of Dr. Bryant. They carried Sean to the Maidu medicine woman who tended to Sean's head wound with warm water and medicinal herbs. Many hours would pass before the white doctor could get to the Maidu village. As the old woman tended his wound, Sean's condition deteriorated. He barely breathed and talked in disjointed phrases which no one could understand.

The Indians sent Ruma to break the news to Finn and his mother. This happened to be the day that Finn walked the orchards with Hannah, explaining the fertilization of their orchards. When Finn heard the news, he took the wagon back to the village with Hannah and found his father comatose, but breathing. He decided to take his father home, and the Indians helped load him into the rear of the wagon on blankets with several more covering him. Hannah sat in the rear with Sean's head on her lap, and Sean's horse was tied to the rear of the wagon. One of the Indian men took a pony and headed for Chico to let the doctor know that Sean was at home.

As Finn pulled the wagon up to the house, Jennifer ran to the wagon at Finn's yell, and the three of them carried Sean into the house. Jennifer cried silently and tended Sean's head wound while they waited for Dr. Bryant. Finn was beside himself and didn't know what to do. He was enraged that his father had been shot and swore revenge while Hannah tried to calm him.

Having been notified that Finn Kerry had taken his wounded father back to their home, Dr. Bryant rode to the Kerry Orchards and began tending Sean. He could see that the wound was serious, and obviously, Jennifer Kerry had done all she could to clean and dress the wicked-looking wound.

Finn looked in on his father while the doctor and his mother tended to Sean. When Dr. Bryant saw him, he directed him out to the hallway while his mother held Sean's hand and Hannah sat in a chair by the window folding sheets. The doctor looked Finn in the eye and shook his head.

'You'd better prepare yourself, Finn. Your pa isn't going to make it. He has a brain injury, and those are usually fatal. His brain is swelling and I'm trying to relieve the pressure, but nothing is working. He's talking, but nothing he says makes any sense. He's raving about gold and Indians and fruit trees and orchards, but I don't understand any of it.'

Finn returned to his father's bedside and sat with him and his mother; Hannah stood behind him with her hands on his shoulders. Once in a while, Sean muttered and waved his arm and talked about waterfalls and pools, but his words didn't make any sense to Finn. Hannah walked past the doctor, saying she would be back in a few minutes.

Still in a rage, Finn considered hunting the killer and killing him himself, but he knew nothing about guns. He remembered the three-shot pistol Sean showed him at one time after Finn arrived, an Allen pistol or some name like that, he thought. He ran to the shed, found the trunk, and lifted the old pistol from its case. Finn turned the weapon over several times as he studied the pistol. The gun looked old and worn. He saw that it had three barrels.

He didn't know how to load it, how to cock it, what kind of ammunition was required or much of anything at all about the dangerous-looking weapon. He knew that if he were to hunt down the man who shot his father, he would have to learn to load, aim, and shoot this pistol. He needed someone to teach him to shoot. He decided that the man who could help him was Hannah's father, Pat, the blacksmith. Working with metals, surely he would know how to handle guns or would know someone who did.

Finn stayed near his father all through the night as the doctor and his mother worked on the head wound. Hannah kept hot water available and washed the sheets and bandages that the doctor continually changed during the course of the night. Toward morning, she finally went to sleep in a chair.

At five in the morning, Sean tried to rise up in bed, saw his son and began to talk.

'Finn, I want to walk outside and see the blue of the mountains in the early morning, feel that warm California breeze and the sun on my skin, and watch the clouds go by. Finn, there's gold in those orchards, so everything will be all right...'

And then he lay back, let out a breath, and died.

Toward sunrise, Hannah woke, gasped as she looked at the quilt that covered Sean's body.

All she could think of at the moment was that Sean was dead.

She wandered outside and found Finn, sitting under an apricot tree, gazing at the sky, tears drying on his cheeks. She went to him and hugged him.

'He's gone, Hannah. What a senseless loss. He tried to save a girl's life and was shot for his efforts. He was such a good man and the best father a man could have. I'll miss him so much.'

They sat quietly holding each other for several minutes, and finally Hannah said, 'So will I.'

By late afternoon of the next day most who knew Sean Kerry had been informed of his death. On her visit to the Maidu village, Hannah informed the Chief.

At home, Finn had made a decision.

'Mother, I am riding into Chico to see Pat Ehrens. I will be back as quickly as I can.'

His mother nodded with hardly a glance at him, still in a daze at the loss of her husband. She sat with her hands in her lap, a bible in her lap. Finn shook his head sadly as he watched his mother, said goodbye to Hannah who sat next to Jennifer and took her hand, and ran to saddle Sean's horse, but found that he was already saddled and standing idle, tied behind the wagon. Finn stroked the old horse and jumped into the saddle.

He rode off at a trot, and headed down the road to Chico.

Pat Ehrens was surprised to see Finn as he rode in on the tired horse. Pat put down his mallet and the horseshoe he had been working on, and walked out to greet Finn.

'Finn, what are you doing in town? You look like hell. Has something happened?'

Finn dismounted and with head hanging turned to Pat.

'Dad's dead, Pat.'

'Dead? Finn, who would shoot your father? Why he's one of the best

89

men I know.'

'Dad was shot trying to help a Maidu Indian girl who was being raped by two white gunmen. The Indians shot one of the men, but they rode off. One's dead now by two Indian arrows, but the other one got away.

'Pat, I want to track down and kill the bastard who shot my father, but I need help. I don't know anything about guns, and I have to learn in a hurry. I have this old three-shot pistol of my father's, but I know nothing about the weapon. Who could teach me what I need to know?'

Pat studied Finn for several seconds and shook his head.

'Finn, you don't want to get involved with guns. Stick with your orchards and let the Sheriff take care of this...'

'Hugh Tindall? What a laugh. Come on, Pat, you know he won't do anything. He can't even handle a rowdy drunk. His deputies do all the hard work. No, this is something I have to do myself. I want to avenge my father's killing. Who can help me? Tell me, Pat. Who can teach me to handle a gun in a hurry?'

Pat glanced around and back at Finn, and shrugged.

'Well, if I wanted to learn about guns, I'd look up Wild Bill Mackey; he's tracked Indians for the army, shot buffalo for hides, and maybe even killed a man or two over the years. He's a weapons dealer these days and you can usually find him hanging out at Palm's Saloon. Of all the men I know who handle firearms, Bill is about the best there is in these parts. I wish you'd change your mind, son, but if not, Bill's your man. I'm sure sorry about your pa. Is your ma okay?'

Finn nodded, left the horse tied to the hitching post in front of the blacksmith shop, and in minutes, he pushed through the swinging doors of Palm's Saloon. He stood in the entrance and scanned the room. Two men sat at one table in the rear, and two more stood at the bar. One of them was talking to the bartender in a loud voice and waving his arms about. Finn walked to the bar, the bartender glanced at him, and stepped over.

'Where can I find Wild Bill Mackey?'

The bartender laughed, pointed to the big man talking and said, 'That's Bill, lad, in the flesh, tellin' us one of his tall tales.' He laughed again and walked back to Bill.

Finn sized up the old gun hand. He was over fifty years old with a rough-looking face, weathered, deeply sunburned, a three-day growth of whiskers, and wearing a worn-out army broad-brimmed hat that had seen better days. His shirt was some kind of fur, and his trousers had a yellow stripe down the outside. Finn noticed his well-worn boots with one foot up on the step at the bottom of the bar. He stepped over and tapped the older man on the shoulder. Bill turned, sized him up, and turned so he was looking right at Finn.

'I'm looking for Bill Mackey. The bartender says that's you.'

Bill smiled and stuck out his hand.

'Wild Bill Mackey's the name. What can I do fer ye, son? Lookin' fer a gun?'

Finn opened the cloth in his hand and brandished the old pistol. Finn heard boots scuffle and chairs scrape the floor as the bartender ducked and the man at the other end of the bar rushed to the other side of the room, spilling beer in the middle of the room.

Before Finn could say another word, he was staring down the barrel of Bill's pistol.

Chapter 15

November 1847

'Whoa, whoa. I just wanted to show you my dad's pistol, Bill. I need someone to teach me to use it, fast. I want to kill the man who killed my pa. And Pat Ehrens said you were the best.'

The room quieted as the men in the bar watched Finn. Bill gave Finn a curious look, a smile appeared on his face, and he slowly put his gun away as he reached over and took the pistol from Finn.

. Bill glanced around the quiet room. He smiled, waved his arms and said, 'its okay, boys, go back to yer drinkin'.' He squinted at Finn.

'You're lookin' to learn to shoot that old Allen Pepperbox pistol? Wal, I reckon I could hep you with that–if you can afford the price of the lessons. But you wanna watch out where you pull that there pistol out, especially in a saloon like Palms. You're apt to get yerself killed afore your gunfight takes place. Let's go sit at a table nice and peaceable like, so's we can figure out how you can go about this. You know anythin' about guns, son?'

Finn shook his head. They sat at the nearest table; the bartender put two beers on the table, and waited to be paid. Bill looked at Finn, and Finn paid for the drinks. Then they got down to business

'Whatever it takes, I'll pay it. But I'm going to kill the dirty bastard that shot my dad. And I'll do whatever it takes to learn how to do it.'

Bill squinted and sized Finn up for the second time, then shook his head.

'Now I don't normal avocate teachin' a man to shoot so's he can gun down another man, but in yer case, I can understand how you feel.

'But there's a lot of learnin' to be done to become a good shooter. If you have the price, I reckon I can teach you what you need to know. You know anything at all about firearms?'

'No, I'm afraid I have never had the opportunity or reason to fire a pistol or rifle.'

'Hmm. Then you're *really* starting from scratch. Where's your home, son?'

'The name is Finn Kerry, and I live with my wife and mother at the Kerry Orchards north of here about twenty miles.'

'Don't get your britches in a crack, Finn. Yeah, I knowed your pa. Sean Kerry, right? Met him at Jon Simms store while I was consignin' some new guns. Right nice fella, your pa. You say someone killed him?'

'Yes, two men tried to rape a Maidu Indian girl and they shot my father. I guess he tried to interfere, but he never carries a gun. The Maidu Indians shot one of the men with arrows. An old prospector named Leggotie was in the area and he saw the two men riding toward the Maidu village before it happened. He rushed to the scene as soon as he heard the shot. Said they were Jasper Biggs and Jed Polk. Biggs took two arrows as he was riding away, but Polk got away leading Biggs on his horse.

'The Indians trailed their horses for a couple of miles and found Biggs lying by a tree, dead with two arrows in him. His pockets were turned out and his gun belt was gone. Guess once Biggs was dead, Polk dumped him and took his gear. Biggs' horse was gone, too. So Polk is also a horse thief, even if Biggs is dead.'

'Hmm,' said Bill. 'Knowed those two fellers. Jed Polk is a gambler among other things and as nasty a character as I've seen and I've seen a few. Saw him playing cards in the backroom here a couple of times. The right side of his face is burned pretty bad, but he tries to cover it with a scraggly beard. This here Polk is a dangerous man, Finn; shifty and quick. He handles a pistol good. He's fast and I hear he killed a man over in Chico last year; pleaded self defense.

'Don't know too much about Biggs, but Sheriff Tindall told me he had Biggs in his little lockup a couple of times for drunkenness and robbery.

'You sure you wanna go after Jed Polk? He's as mean as they come, Finn.'

'Yes, I want to kill the bastard as soon as I can learn to use a gun and find him. So what do I have to do?'

'Okay, Finn. First off, I saw you ride in on that old horse, so I suppose you may be needin' a better horse if we're gonna track Polk down 'cause you may be on the road a spell. Go see Mort Persons at the livery stables. Tell him I sent you and he'll sell you a good saddle-broke horse for about one hundred dollars. Your saddle may be good enough, but you're gonna need saddle bags to keep your gear in and food and an extra shirt and pants and underwear and a bed roll among other things.'

He picked up Finn's gun from the table.

'This old Allen Pepperbox pistol has three barrels, no sights, takes a 31 caliber ball and I see it's made for a percussion cap which is good. But, Finn, this takes a powerful trigger pull 'cause you're rotating all three cylinders, cocking the hammer, and firing the pistol all in one trigger squeeze. Takes right powerful fingers to handle that gun and you won't be able to keep that gun pointin' straight at your target with all that trigger squeezin' takin' place.

'So you want a gun that will be stable while you're aiming at your target, and my recommendation would be to get a Colt Baby Dragoon. They call it a Pocket Pistol 'cause it's easy to conceal, and it fits in a holster fine, too. That shoots a 31 caliber ball like yer Allen, and uses percussion caps with fifty grain powder loads. But no matter, it's still a bear to *load*–not shoot, but load; when you're ready to shoot at your target, you'll have five shots with that Colt before you have to reload, more than enough for a gun fight; however, you do need to cock that hammer for each shot, but you'll get used to that pretty quick. This here Colt pocket pistol is the preferred gun of every man who carries a weapon on his hip today.

'This Baby Colt is the gun you want, and I happen to have three available right fresh from the factory. And these are the first ones with the load lever built into the front under the barrel. That makes seating the ball lots easier when you have to load. And I can let you have your choice for thirty-five dollars.

'Okay, next is your ammunition. If you go with the Pocket Pistol, that takes 31 caliber balls and percussion caps, and I have plenty of those. Oh yeah, and wads to help seat the balls in the cylinder chambers. You're going to need lots of ammo to practice with this gun before you'll be ready for any shootouts, let me tell you. You'll get plenty of practice cleaning this Baby, too, once you start shootin'.

'Then you'll need a holster for that gun and a gun belt. If you're plannin' for a shootout, you won't be needin' more than the five-shot load of a single cylinder, but you will be needin' a leather thong to tie that holster to your leg so you can draw easy and smooth; however, for practice I'd recommend an extra cylinder so you can have ten shots available while you practice. You won't need but one in a shootout. I don't know of any one-on-one gun fights where either man needed more than two or three shots before it's all over, although I got to say, ain't many one-on-one duels anymore. Just so's you know what you're gettin' into.'

'And I noticed that short-billed cap you're wearin'. I would advise you to get a wide-brimmed hat so's the sun don't blind you before the big shootout. If yer facin' the sun, it'll help shade your eyes from the sun's glare, too, a good thing in a gunfight. But one of the things I teach you is to always–*always*–get the sun behind you in a showdown. Let the other feller squint at the sun. Gives you a big edge, Finn. Bear that in mind.

'And as I mentioned, you'll need some trail gear, too: A bed roll, slicker, gloves, coffee pot and tin cup, flint and steel for startin' fires, and a tin plate to eat your food in. If you like sugar in your coffee, bring that, and salt if you want, and flour or cornmeal for breakfast cakes and…'

Finn threw up his hands.

'Whoa, Bill. You sure I don't want a *wagon* and mule instead of a horse with all this gear you're telling me I need? I guess I never realized there'd be so much involved. I'll have to think on this a while. This may run into more money than I've got right at the moment. I just got married, and I'm trying to make a home for my new wife, so that'll take some money, too.'

Bill chuckled and eyed Finn with curiosity.

'Don't tell me *you're* the fella that's married Hannah Ehrens.'

Finn smiled broadly.

'Yep, that's me, Bill.'

'Wal, now, you got one sweet girl there. Hmm, maybe we'd better forget about this gun totin', Finn. I wouldn't want to get you into something that would make her a widow. Pat Ehrens would never forgive me.'

Finn gave Bill a nasty look.

'No matter what you say, Bill, I'm going to find and kill Jed Polk and that's that. It's either him or me. So tell me what I need to do.'

'Okay, Finn. Calm down.' He thought a moment. 'Do you suppose your ma could put up with me for a few weeks? I could bring my gear out to the orchards and we could find us a place to practice there, and if you have a hayloft, I can sleep right there, too.'

'Yes, that would work. And I could spend some time in the orchards tending the trees and mending fences when I'm not shooting at targets.'

Bill glanced at Finn oddly.

'Yeah...well, okay, bring your wagon into town tomorrow early, and we'll load up and take everything to your house. Is your ma a good cook, Finn?'

Finn laughed. 'As good as you'll find anywhere, and she loves cooking for strangers, too. Wait'll you taste her apple pie. My wife, Hannah, is a good cook, too.'

Bill smiled a toothy grin.

'This may work out good for both of us, Finn. If their cookin's as good as you say, maybe I might knock off a few dollars on those lessons.'

Finn then left in a hurry and rode home to be with his family.

Chapter 16

November 1847

Three days later Sean Kerry's funeral was held at his home. Sean was laid out in a mahogany coffin, and the people who came walked past him, maybe said a prayer, and sat down. Hannah stood staring down at Sean, held back tears, and gritted her teeth. Finn stood in front of his father for a long time, tears on his cheeks, as he clenched and unclenched his fists.

'I swear to you, Dad, that I will punish the man who did this.'

An old stranger approached Finn before the burial.

'I'm Cal Matlock, a store owner in Chico, Mr. Kerry. You might not remember me. This may not be the right time to talk of this, but I knew the Polk family; they were a bad lot, all of them. Jed had at least two brothers that I know of. They were bad as Jed, maybe worse. I heard that one brother poured kerosene on Jed when he was ten and threw a match. The other brother tried to put it out, but one side of Jed's face was badly burned. You can't miss that dark shriveled skin if you look at the man.

'After that, Jed turned real mean. He couldn't find a woman who would have him, so he took up cards and did right well, although some say he cheated a lot. I don't know about that, but he did seem to be awful lucky. The surprising part is, usually Jed is an amiable fella. He has charm when he wants to, but if he's riled, he can be as mean as a cornered cougar.

'Just so's you know, Mr. Kerry. Jed Polk is a terror with a gun. He's fast and he's killed one man at the card tables that I know of, and wounded a couple of other fellas, too. I even heard he dry-gulched a man who beat him at cards. Best be careful if you're a-thinkin' about calling him out.

'Thanks for the information, Mr. Matlock. I'll bear that in mind.'

'Sorry about your father.'

Sean was buried on a hillside behind the house near one of his favorite oak trees on a cold mid-morning November day. The gathering included Finn and Hannah, Finn's mother, Pat Ehrens, Jon Simms from the general store, Dr. Bryant from Chico, several Chico store owners, Sheriff Tindall and one deputy, the eight Maidu Indian boys and their parents, Chief Sam, and the Methodist minister. The service was short and Finn said a few words about his father.

'My father was a good man. I doubt that he ever had an enemy. His passion in life was his fruit orchards and growing things. He told me once that Nature was a tool of God, and he spent his life learning to use that tool for the nourishment of everybody through the plants he grew.

'Those who knew my father will feel a great loss in his passing.'

When he finished, Jennifer sprinkled dirt on the casket, the Maidu Indian boys shoveled dirt onto the wooden top, and said a few Indian words over the grave. Then the Indians left and the rest adjourned to the house to console Jennifer, talk about Sean, and get refreshments furnished by Jennifer Kerry and Hannah.

Sheriff Tindall approached Finn on the front porch.

'Finn, Jed Polk disappeared. You may not know that Polk wounded one of my deputies when he tried to arrest him after the shooting of your father. No one's seen him since your father was killed. He's probably left the area by now. That ornery rat was just too quick with that gun of his. Polk gathered his gambling money and his gear and took off. I'm sorry about Sean.'

In his mind Finn was furious. He knew that this inept sheriff would do nothing; justice for Sean Kerry rested with me. Learning to use a gun is my first priority now. Tindall was too busy working behind the scenes for John Bidwell who owned much property along the Feather River. Tindall was at Bidwell's beck and call.

Early in November, Sheriff Tindall was replaced in the election by

Bob Clayton, who had been a lawman for twenty years, and wasn't working for Bidwell.

With his mother's agreement, Finn took over the operation of the Kerry Orchards, but Finn had Jed Polk on his mind, and nothing would deter him from seeking out and killing the man.

Chapter 17

December 1847

After looking over the Kerry orchards, Bill Mackey picked a spot far from the house and out of sight of any people, as he had noticed the Maidu Indian boys at work in the orchard. He stored his gear in the shed and he and Finn rode out to the spot where Bill laid out several pistols.

'These two on the left are Colt Baby Dragoons with 31 caliber balls and percussion caps; the cap holds yer powder charge of about 50 grains. That one on the right is an original Colt Dragoon six-shooter. Notice the longer barrel. That's fourteen and a quarter inches long, compared to eight and a quarter long on the Baby. The Dragoon is not a gun you could easily put in a holster on your hip; most fellers carry that hog in a horse holster. For one thing it's too heavy at four-and-a-half pounds to carry around, and for another you'd never be able to draw that artillery out of a gun holster with that long barrel. You'd be dead before you cleared your holster. The Dragoon uses a 44 caliber ball and is hell on the man who is hit with it. But you don't need that size ball to put a man down, Finn.

'So we're gonna be firing this Baby Colt; that's my recommendation, Finn. Some folks call it a Pocket Pistol 'cause you can easily conceal it in a pocket. It weighs just over two pounds, has a four-inch barrel, and is much shorter than that Dragoon, and you can right nicely nest it in a holster on your hip. The big Dragoon took the place of the old Colt Walker pistol with its fifteen and a half-inch length because they both fired a deadly 44 caliber missile which was accurate up to about thirty yards, but the Walker had bad problems because of the powder load of 60 grains; sometimes it would explode because the barrel wasn't made for that big a charge. Lotta fingers and eyes got lost with the Walker. This Baby pistol uses forty-five to fifty grain loads, so it's easier on the metal parts.

'I want you to carry the unloaded Baby around with you in this holster for the next fifteen to twenty days so's you get the feel of it. Pull it out and cock the hammer as much as possible so you get the feel of the weight and balance, and train your hand and arm to pulling this out of a holster. Your thumb needs lots of exercise cocking that hammer, and you have to learn to cock it while your arm is coming up with the gun out of yer holster. You won't feel the full weight like when it's loaded, but you'll feel like that gun is part of you pretty quick. As I said, this here's a five-shot pistol with a 31 caliber ball, just like your old Allen Pepperbox pistol.

'Okay, Finn, let me show you how to load this Baby.'

Bill placed the rear of the pistol butt on the wooden table and pulled the hammer back part way.

'First, you put the hammer on half cock like this; you give the trigger a little squeeze to bring the hammer to half cock. That frees up the cylinder so's you can rotate it to each ball position. Now you put this wad on the chamber of the cylinder opening and lay the ball on top of it. Then you use the load lever, which is the crank you see there under the barrel. You line up the lever end with the cylinder, and push the wad and ball fully into the cavity with the lever till it seats.

'The wad is important because ammunition is not always perfectly sized to the barrel. Without the wad, a ball could simply roll out the barrel before you are ready to fire, so the wad kinda packs the ball into the hole snug-like without binding the ball.

'And the last step in loading is to insert the percussion cap on that little threaded tit sticking out the rear of the cylinder. Your cap has the right amount of gun powder built into it, and when you pull the trigger, the hammer whacks the cap in the rear; the powder explodes, goes through a little flash hole behind the wad and ball, and forces the ball out of the pistol at a tolerable rate of speed.

Okay, now the gun is loaded, and by squeezing the trigger while holding the hammer, you ease that hammer down and you're ready to fire. Now you load this Baby Colt. Here is the wad, balls, and caps.'

Finn loaded the Colt and with the first ball made clumsy mistakes. But after loading several chambers in the cylinder, he had the hang of it and snickered.

'I assume you always load this pistol before you're ready for action, right?'

Bill laughed. 'That's the idea, Finn. You always have a full five shots in the cylinder before the action starts. Otherwise, you're a dead man.

'Okay, one more thing. You can carry a loaded cylinder as a spare; a lot of soldiers do that so they have ten shots available in a hurry in a battle. Here's how you change cylinders. First you tap this metal wedge on the right side of the pistol to unseat it, and pull out the wedge from the left side. This separates the barrel from the rear of the pistol. Take care you don't lose that metal wedge, or you can't put the gun back together. I always put the wedge in the barrel while I have the pistol apart.'

Bill tapped the wedge with the handle of his big knife, and the wedge broke free. Bill pulled it out and slipped the barrel off the end of the gun.

'See the rod sticking out, Finn? That's what guides the barrel into position along its axis. Now that the barrel is out of the way, you can slip the used cylinder off the gun and replace it with a loaded one. Then you put the barrel back on, insert the wedge and give it a light tap to seat it well, and you're ready to fire again with another five rounds.'

'Okay, Bill, we have two loaded cylinders with one on the gun. Show me how to shoot this thing.'

Bill laughed, and then got serious.

'First off, never point at anything you don't mean to shoot, especially me. Now let's fire at the targets I've set up out there by that old tree. As you can guess, you wanna hit that center bull's eye as many times as you can out of five shots before you have to reload. We're about thirty-five feet away.

'And here's something I'm gonna teach you right off. You have the perfect build for a gun fighter; you're slim and lanky, and if you stand sideways to your opponent, you will make a dam hard target to hit. So do all your shooting standing sideways till you're used to it. And just rest your unused hand on your hip.

'What's the trick to aiming this gun, Bill? I've never done this before.'

'Nothin' to it, Finn. See,' he said, handling the gun, 'you have this vertical blade front sight and a hammer notch rear sight. What you do is find your target, put the front blade sight right under it and bring the blade into the center of the hammer notch. You should be in the center bull's eye every time if you do that.' He laughed. 'Well, that's the theory, anyway.'

Finn took the pistol, stood sideways to the target, raised the weapon with his left hand, and lined up the blade and notch on the center spot as Bill said. He pulled the trigger, but nothing happened, and he looked at Bill in confusion. Bill laughed.

'Oh, yes. Maybe I forgot to tell you. You have to cock the hammer before each shot. Try it again. I just noticed that you're left-handed.'

'Yep, been a lefty all my life. Does that make any difference, Bill?'

'No, no. I guess I haven't seen too many left-handed shooters is all.'

Finn cocked the hammer with difficulty, stood sideways, raised the pistol, and slowly pulled the trigger. The explosion almost made Finn drop the gun, his arm kicked back, and he lost his balance as he was surrounded by smoke and the smell of gun powder.

'You didn't tell me the gun would knock *me* down, too.'

He placed the gun on the wooden table and followed Bill to the target thirty-five feet away. They looked at the target, but no holes were evident. Bill shrugged.

'You'll get the hang of it, Finn. That was your first shot. Don't expect miracles. Try it again. And remember to *squeeze that trigger slow* while watching the target. Don't let your trigger squeeze throw you off the target. And one other thing. Placin' your right hand on your right hip is correct, but as yer sightin', your right elbow tends to stick out from behind your side. You want to make yourself as small a target as you can.'

On the second shot they found a hole in the third ring around the center.

'Much better, Finn. You're gettin' there. Remember squeeze that trigger slow so it don't throw you off the target.'

'Yes, I see how pulling the trigger moves me off the black spot. I'll try to compensate for that next time.'

Bill looked at him, nodded, and made a wry smile.

The third shot was a miss, and Finn showed his frustration. Bill touched Finn's shoulder.

'Listen to these words of wisdom, Finn. Practice makes perfect. That's your mantra from now on. *Practice makes perfect.*'

Finn clipped the target outside of all the rings on the fourth shot.

'Squeeze, Finn, and slow. And keep that right arm behind you. You're stickin' your elbow out too far. Keep your right elbow in line with your body.'

Finn's fifth shot was off the center by one inch, and Bill smiled with surprise.

'Now that's shootin', Finn. Remember what you did on that last shot. Get that picture in your mind. Now change barrels the way I showed you and do it again. You have five more shots.

The first shot with the new cylinder was inside the fourth ring. The second shot was close to the bull's eye.

Three more shots put holes in the second ring and Bill showed his uneven teeth.

Finn changed cylinders again and took his position while Bill hung a new target.

Finn's first shot put a hole in the edge of the target sheet, the next three shots were all in the second ring, and his last shot put a hole in the opposite side of the sheet.

Bill looked at the target, and scrutinized Finn with his hands on his broad hips.

'Okay, Finn, now you need to relax and think on what you're doing. The squeeze and aim is the most important part of being a gun fighter, Finn. Let's call it a day and you can practice drawing and squeezing while you aim. Tomorrow you will do better after a night's sleep and plenty of thinking about that gun and how to handle it.'

Chapter 18

November 1847

The next day they started at sunrise, with light fog still on the ground around them. Bill set up the targets and walked back to Finn.

'I see you loaded both cylinders. Good. That'll give you ten shots to get started. I'm supplyin' you with two more cylinders so's you can get off twenty shots before you reload.

'You ready?'

Finn nodded, took a sideways stance to the target, and pulled the pistol while cocking the hammer. In the same motion his arm came up, he sighted, let out a breath, and squeezed the trigger.'

The explosion didn't bother Finn today. Bill Mackey nodded with a smile.

'You're a fast learner. You must have done a heap of thinkin' on this last night. Now for the important part. Let's see if you hit anything.'

They walked to the target and Bill let out a loud 'Yes! You done clipped the edge of the second ring, Finn. Nice shootin'.'

On the next four shots, Finn hit inside the second ring twice, hit inside the third ring once, and nicked the edge of the bull's eye once.

'No doubt about it; you're improvin'. Let's put on a new cylinder.'

Finn changed cylinders and fired five more shots at a new target.

'Bill, I feel like I'm getting control over the squeeze-and-aim. Let's see whether the target says what I think it should.'

They walked to the target.

'Damn, you *are* comin' right along; one in the second ring, three in the first ring, and one where half the ball went through the bull. Good shootin'. I think you need to wait now and take some time for lunch. Yer Ma says she's havin' country sausage, biscuits, mashed taters, and green beans today for lunch. Don't reckon we can disappoint the lady, can we?'

They both laughed, and Finn studied the gun for a moment, and then put the Colt on the table and covered everything with a piece of canvas.

That afternoon, Finn fired one cylinder of five shots; put three close to the bull's eye, and the other two in the second ring. Bill looked at the target with surprise.

'Finn, are you funnin' me, boy? You sure you never fired a gun before?'

Finn shrugged.

'No, this is my first time, honest. Am I doing better, Bill?'

'Unless this was an accident, this is your best shootin' yet. Kid, if you could shoot like you did with these last three shots, there would be a dead man layin' in the sun. Let's see you put that new loaded cylinder on the pistol.'

Finn tapped the wedge loose, pulled it out of the side of the gun, and removed the barrel. He slid off the used cylinder and put the new loaded one on the gun, replaced the barrel, and inserted and seated the metal wedge.

'Good boy, Finn. You're getting the hang of this quick.'

With a new target in place, Finn cocked the pistol, took his stance, raised the pistol, aimed for the center spot, and slowly squeezed the trigger. The sound was deafening, but Finn now knew what to expect. He waved away the smoke and walked to the target with Bill.

'Wal, I'll be...' Bill said. '

You just got yerself a bull's eye, Finn. Let's see you do that agin. Land a-goshin', but you are learnin' fast.'

Finn fired four more times, hit two more bulls eyes, put one in the third ring from the bull, and one on the line between the third and fourth rings from the bull.

Bill slapped his leg with his hat.

'By dam, I think you're a natural. I don't know too many men can shoot that good after *years* of experience. Are you doin' just what I told you?'

Finn nodded. 'Yes, I think the trick is keeping that target on the blade and notch like you said, and then being slow on that trigger squeeze. I noticed a couple of times I pulled the trigger too fast and the trigger pull threw me off a tad. When I squeeze the trigger slowly, I never know when it will release the hammer, so I can concentrate on aiming at that target.'

Bill was laughing so hard he almost fell over.

'We best be getting back to the house for dinner. Your ma said she was havin' chicken and dumplin's tonight.'

He looked at the sun slowly dropping toward the hills.

'That's enough practice for a start. We'll start fresh tomorrow...after you tend your trees. I think you ma is making flapjacks for breakfast tomorrow, and I don't want to miss out on that.'

Finn laughed as he mounted his horse. 'You sure do like your vitals, Bill.'

* * *

The next morning as usual, Bill and Finn rode out to the practice spot, and Bill took the pistol from Finn's holster.

'Before we start tearin' up targets today, these cylinders need a good cleanin'. Now I ain't said much about cleanin' yet, but it's somethin' you need to know. Every good gun handler cleans his gun after every shootin' session. That way nothin' bad happens to you or your gun when you're shootin' away for real.

'Now we have two dirty cylinders here, so let me show you how to clean them. First you gotta take the gun apart, and you need the right tools for this here Pocket Pistol.

'You need a nipple wrench like this one, a flathead screwdriver, and somethin' with a little heft to it like a mallet or a big knife like mine with a metal handle so's you can give that wedge a good tap to free it. I'll throw in the tools and you find yerself a good heavy-handled knife.

'As I said yesterday, once you loosen the wedge, you pull it out of the left side like this. Then you can remove the barrel, like so. If the barrel is on real tight, I use the lever to push on the cylinder to break it free. You have to put the hammer on half-cock so's you can rotate the cylinder

107

between chambers. Then push on it with the lever and it'll pop a stuck barrel free. I always put the wedge into the barrel so's I don't lose it. '

He laid the barrel on the wooden table and continued.

'Clean the barrel outside parts and then swab out the bore. This keeps your barrel from gettin' rusty when it's not in use. Swabbing the bore makes sure there's no dirt or other debris inside to distract that ball from sliding out the barrel. The inside should look kinda shiny. Then unscrew the nipples from the cylinder for cleanin'. Use this here light oil on all parts and wipe almost dry. That gives your gun rust protection. I always grease the nipple threads before putting it back. That stops the charge from blowing back at you and adds extra energy to force the ball forward.

'Use something like a nail or a small wood rod and push a wad to the bottom of the chamber, and then rotate it while pushing on the rod to loosen any debris that's clingin' to the back of the chamber near the flash hole. Be sure to unblock those flash holes. You have to keep them clean for good performance.

'And that's about it. Then you just put everythin' back together pretty much like you took it apart, and make sure that wedge is in snug by giving it a little whack to seat it good.

'Now we've been using two cylinders since you don't want to disrupt yer shooting every five shots. A good shooter will usually carry at least two cylinders, so's he can change over quick when he's in a battle situation, and an experienced gun toter can replace that cylinder in about ten seconds. Wal, you don't need two cylinders, since you're gonna be in a one-on-one gun fight with that Polk feller, and five shots with the aim you're developin' will be more than enough. Okay, your gun's back together and loaded, so let's see you hit that center spot some more. Just remember that loadin' a new cylinder requires the barrel assembly to be taken off so the old cylinder can be slipped out and the new one slipped in. Then the barrel assembly is replaced and wedged.'

Finn nodded and took his sideways position, put his right hand on his hip with his elbow behind him, pulled the pistol out of the holster, cocked the hammer as he raised his arm, all in a smooth fluid motion. He sighted on the target, squeezed the trigger as he breathed out slowly, and fired, sending up a cloud of smoke around him.

With his arm raised Finn cocked the hammer, sighted, and fired again. He did this three more times, and then slipped the pistol smoothly back in the holster.

Bill watched him throughout this round of shooting.

'Lordy, Finn, I swear I was watching a professional gun slinger the way you handled that gun. Your draw was smooth and pretty quick, you cocked that hammer easier than you did yesterday, and you didn't flinch when that gun fired. If you can handle yourself like that in a gun fight, then you'll be the better man.'

Finn nodded.

'I tried something new today. First, I kept my arm raised and cocked the hammer each time, and second, I let out my breath slowly as I was aiming; seems to keep me steadier, Bill.'

'Yes, if you can cock that hammer with your arm raised, you save time. I've seen other men do that. With some guns they call that fannin', but they aren't aiming so much as pointing and shooting. If it works for you, do it, I say, but always *aim* that pistol.

'Now lemme say one more thing about this gun fightin', Finn. There's gonna be a feller lookin' at you and aimin' at you and shootin' at you as fast as he can. Don't let that rattle you. Before you draw your weapon, shake out yer arms and wrists. Get loosened up so's yer actions are fast and precise. But once't you pull that gun and aim, don't let that other man's first shot disturb you if he's faster than you. Keep calm, and squeeze that trigger like you've been doing, and I guarantee, your first shot will kill him.

'And, by the way, you have two good places to aim; one is the head and the other is the heart. Most gun toters aim for the heart, 'cause it seems like a bigger target, but it ain't. The head is bigger than the heart. If you hit either one of those on your first shot, he's a dead man. So pick your spot, stay calm, and squeeze that trigger. Okay, let's take a look at how you did on that target.'

They walked to the target, and Bill bent slightly to look at it.

'Hell's bells, Finn. You done put three shots on the edge of the center bull's eye and two in the second ring. Man, you're a shootist, Finn. You're on your way to your goal. You just keep practicin' the motions you used today and hittin' that center spot and you'll get your man when the time comes. Lordy, Lordy. I can't believe what I'm seein'. You have some eye.'

He took the pistol from Finn, covered their ammunition, and they walked back to the house.

As they sat on the porch later enjoying Jennifer's lemonade, Bill brought up a new subject.

'Finn, I've about shown you all I can about that Colt Baby Dragoon, and I think you'll agree that it's a great pistol for the person who knows how to handle it. But let's think on this subject of guns a bit further.

Chapter 19

November 1847

'Sometime in your future you're gonna find yourself at a distance from your target, and in those cases you're gonna need a rifle since even your Pocket Pistol only has a range of about twenty-five to thirty yards. Now I know you said your daddy has this old Kentucky muzzle-loader that was converted to percussion caps, and that's all well and good. But that Kentucky rifle went through some *other* changes as time passed, and I want to introduce you to these changes on one of my favorites.

'I have several rifles I sell which can do a right fine job, like the Winchester lever-action, the Springfield Muskatoon, and my all-time favorite, this Kentucky rifle.

'Of all these choices, I recommend the Kentucky rifle over others because of its accuracy. At two-hundred yards, you just can't beat that devil–as long as it's been modified correctly and has a good shooter behind the sights. That's you, Finn.

'Let me show you this rifle. See? It looks almost like yer daddy's rifle, but there are improvements in this here rifle you want to be aware of.

I have two Kentucky rifles I had modified to fire a .31 caliber ball. It's lighter than most Kentuckys and it means if I carry a Baby Dragoon, I always have plenty of ammo for both guns. You can even keep your wads or patches in the stock in a special cabinet.

'First off it has been converted to the percussion ball and cap, just like yer daddy's. This rifle is designed to be graceful, slender, and light. It fires a .31 caliber ball, has a forty-inch barrel, and has been rifled with helical grooving.

'Now let's look at these improvements separately. First the percussion cap conversion. In a battle that percussion cap pays for itself in its trustworthiness. With the old flint-lock mechanism, the rifle might misfire on a wet day; you don't get that problem with the percussion cap system. Yer powder is high and dry every time.

'By changing to a .31 caliber ball, you automatically save weight in yer ammunition, and that means you can carry more ammo 'thout getting a hernia. And as I said, if you also carry the Colt Baby Dragoon, you have ammo for both guns.

'That forty-inch barrel was added for a good reason. When yer powder explodes, it moves out the barrel and expands till it's free of the gun barrel, and there's yer difference; with the longer barrel, that powder *keeps* expanding longer and gives your ball an extra punch. This extends your accurate firing range somewhat, too. Why, in the hands of a good shooter, yer range might be as much as three-hundred yards. 'Course, that's pushin' it a bit.

'As for riflin' the barrel with that helical groove, gun makers found in testing that a rifled barrel gave a spiral twist to the ball and kept it from deviatin' from the target. Without that riflin' the ball might travel in a slight curve, and you may miss your target altogether. Riflin' compensates for the small imperfections in the bore of yer barrel. So puttin' the riflin' together with the longer barrel gives you both more accuracy and range.

'Now gun owners are particular 'bout their guns. Some have elaborate decorations all over the stocks and some even decorate their barrels. Wal, I don't care much about the fancy trim as long as my hog shoots straight and long when I'm a-needin' it.

'So tomorrow, yer gonna fire that modified Kentucky and see what you can do with it.'

Finn agreed and looked the rifle over as they took a refill of lemonade.

Early the next morning they were back at their target spot, only Bill stepped off a two-hundred yard distance to the target.

'Okay, Finn. Since this is a single-shot rifle, you have to reload after every round. So shoot five shots at that two-hundred-yard target and let's see how you do. Remember to consider the wind direction and try to compensate in your aim. Go to it.'

Finn used his usual technique of breathing out and squeezing the trigger, and then reloaded four more times.

'Now let's see what damage you did.'

They walked to the target and studied the hits.

'No surprise to me, Finn. You hit the target five times which is great. But see? Your hits are all grouped together in the left-bottom part of the target. You need to compensate for elevation and wind next time.

'And by the way, a good target-shooter with a Kentucky will generly clean the barrel after two shots, 'cause that long barrel gathers a lot of debris when you shoot. You'll begin to lose accuracy if you don't clean the bore after every two shots.

Finn shot another five rounds, and they walked to the target.

'By dam!' exclaimed Bill. 'You have some kinda eye there, Finn. You done grouped five shots in a space just below the bull's eye. Wow! Come on. Let's see you do it again.'

As they walked back, Finn could hear Bill chuckling to himself and murmuring words he couldn't catch.

Finn shot five more rounds, and they walked to the target. Bill studied the target and was silent for a moment.

'You have five hits grouped right around that there bull's eye; three of them is touchin' the bull. I have to tell you, Finn. I have never seed a shooter with your eye before. Why you could win prizes with yer shootin'. I guess you've shot that there Kentucky rifle enough,' he said as he walked away holding up the target.

'Now we have to cover one more subject. It's not somethin' I like to think on, but you best be prepared for anything in a duel.

'What if your shootin' arm or hand was hit? What would you do?'

Finn thought for a moment.

'I'd probably die.' He laughed. 'I'm kidding, Bill. I guess I'd switch hands.'

'Right! So that means we have to find out how good you can shoot with your right hand since you're a lefty. Now I brought a right-handed holster with me today just on the outside chance that we might get around to this subject. Put this holster on your gun belt and lift your pistol a few times to get the feel of it.'

Finn slipped the holster onto his gun belt, put his pistol in it and tried drawing a few times. At first this felt awkward, and he knew he'd have to practice a right-hand draw in order to get smoother.

'Okay, Finn, let's shoot five. Jist draw, cock, aim, and fire like you allays do.'

Finn fired off five rounds.

'Sure feels awkward, Bill. But I think I can get the hang of it. My trigger finger is not as strong as my left one. Neither is my thumb. I'll have to work on that. And I may not be holding my aim while I'm pulling the trigger.'

'That's right, Finn. Your cocking thumb needs work and your trigger finger needs work. Let's see what you did to the target. Don't be surprised at a few misses.'

They walked to the target.

'Wal, coulda been worse. You hit in the second ring twice which is good, but you have three strays there that hit in the fourth ring near the edge of the target. So your trigger finger is movin' the barrel off the target. You'll have to work on that.

'Now here's what I recommend. Switch hands every other day till you smooth out your aim and trigger pull. Shoot lefty one day, righty the next. It'll take you a while. But I wouldn't want to send you into a gun fight with one arm tied behind your back, so to speak.'

And in succeeding days Finn alternated hands. His shooting never equaled his left-hand shooting, but he improved his draw and cock, and continuously put his shots in the second ring or bull's eye.

* * *

Finn invited Bill Mackey to their home to celebrate Thanksgiving, an arbitrary day toward the end of November, celebrated by the Kerry family for decades.

Jennifer and Hannah worked all morning to prepare a huge turkey, fruits, mashed potatoes, and giblet gravy, savory corn saved from the last harvest, assorted vegetables, and wine.

Hannah was in her fourth month of pregnancy and Finn smiled and patted her tummy twice during the festivities. He hugged her tightly and gave her a long, soft kiss before the meal got underway. Finally when everyone was seated at the table, Finn rose and spoke.

'Let's bow our heads and pray,' said Finn and he said a long prayer of thanksgiving for all their blessings during the year. At the end he commemorated their celebration to Sean Kerry who had always observed Thanksgiving during Finn's life and taught him to be thankful for the bounties the Lord had bestowed on their family.

'In closing, I'd like to thank the Lord for our new child who will be coming sometime in March. And just so you're aware, most of our plant-based foods came from the wonderful garden that Mom and Hannah have been tending with such care all through the year.

'Amen,' said everyone.

Bill Mackey had several helpings of turkey, dressing, mashed potatoes, and vegetables, and finished off the meal with a huge glass of wine.

By mid-afternoon everyone was a bit lethargic from the heavy foods, and before long Bill and Finn were napping while Jennifer and Hannah cleaned up.

The day was a great success.

Chapter 20

December 1847

Twelve days later in the second week of December, Bill Mackey was ready to end the lessons. He had done everything he could think of for Finn Kerry, and Finn had done the rest. In Bill's opinion, Finn was a first class shootist with an eye for a target like Bill had never seen before.

'Don't think there's much else I can teach you, Finn. You hit that bull's eye better'n most men I know, and your draw and cock is smooth. You seem calm when you aim and fire, and that's important.

'One more thing I feel I oughta mention to you. I'm sure you're aware that dueling between two men is mostly against the law; it all depends on the town where it happens. The best advice I can give you about the man who shot your pa is this: Forget the one-on-one duel. You'd be risking your life when there are better ways of killing scum like Polk. Shoot him when he's not expecting it, or catch him in an alley somewhere. That code of the west you mentioned is fine for books and such, but the truth is that few men adhere to it; rather, dry-gulch the bastard when he's not aware of you. Now I know you're one a them purists who figures you owe the other guy an even break. Personally for a killer like Polk I compare him to a filthy rat, and would shoot him on sight, but I know you won't do that, so all I can say is good luck.

'And one other thing I should say. I don't know anythin' about Jed Polk, but lots of folks have kin, and kin can get mighty riled when one of their relatives gets killed. So if you do kill Jed Polk, you'd best watch your back, Finn.

'Yes, a merchant from Chico told me that Jed Polk has at least two brothers.'

Bill squinted and said, 'Then like I said, you'd best watch yer back.

'Reckon I'm going to collect my gear and mosey back to town, see if Simm's has sold any of my new guns. That there Baby Dragoon is yours if you want it. And I'll sell you one of my modified Kentucky rifles with the .31 caliber barrel, too. And I'll throw in two hundred balls and caps in the bargain. You still need to gather the equipment I mentioned. I made a list for you. Don't skimp on any of your gear, and when we're out on the road tracking Polk, you'll be glad you bought the best. It will make your life more pleasant.

'Lucky I got that advance on royalties for my book, Bill. That gave me enough money to get all this equipment a horse, and pay you for lessons, too.'

'I gotta tell you though,' said Bill, 'I'm gonna miss your ma's cookin'. You were right. She's some cook. Your wife, too.'

'Thanks for all your help teaching me how to use guns, Bill. I'll see you in Chico tomorrow morning when I bring my wagon in to collect all the gear on that list you gave me, and to get a new horse from Person. Is there anything special I should know about buying a horse?'

'No, just tell Mort I sent you and he'll treat you right. Known him a long time and he's a fair man.'

Within three days Finn had his new horse, named him Blue, and bought all the equipment on the list Bill had provided. Hannah watched him as he spent time cleaning his new gear and packing most of it in his new saddle bags for the trail. Hannah knew the time was almost here when Finn and Bill would be leaving to track Sean's killer.

* * *

A light sprinkling of dry snow had fallen on Christmas Eve, and by mid-morning of Christmas day, the women were busy in the kitchen preparing a Christmas feast. Their efforts outdid the Thanksgiving dinner, if that was possible, and everyone, including Bill Mackey, was stuffed with good food and wine at dinner.

Hannah was now in her fifth month of pregnancy and appeared

healthy and fit. Finn took every opportunity to attend to her, kissing and hugging her from time to time during the entire day, and watching her carefully as she moved about the room serving everyone.

At the end of their dinner, the group gathered around the small Christmas tree that Finn had cut down. The tree was decorated with colorful paper chains, tinsel, pine cones, and small candles, all lit for the celebration.

A few presents were exchanged with 'ooh's and 'ahh's.

Jennifer had made a quilted blanket for Bill Mackey who, by this time, occupied the guest bedroom.

Bill had made a baby crib with carvings on every leg.

Finn had given Hannah a beautiful blue robe to wear on cold mornings.

After the presents were opened, Finn played the flute for a while as everyone sipped their drinks and listened. The women sang along with some of Finn's tunes.

During the afternoon, Finn took Hannah aside and explained the trip that he and Bill were about to take to find Jed Polk, Sean's killer. She understood perfectly now and understood the determination of her husband to avenge his father's killing. She didn't want him to go, but she resigned herself not to show her emotions.

* * *

Early in the morning of the day he and Bill were to leave to track down Jed Polk, Finn sat on the edge of the bed and watched his wife, Hannah, as she lay sleeping. Was he being fair to her? He wondered. He knew he could be killed in this undertaking. He hoped she understood the obligation to his father. He had to avenge his murder. If he were killed, he would never see his new child. Was killing Jed Polk worth it? He gritted his teeth as he thought of the killer. Damn him, he thought, as he lay back down, turned to the quiet form of the woman he loved, and put his hand over hers. She had made him so happy. He hoped he wasn't ignoring his new family. He wrote Hannah a short love note and quietly left their room.

They rode out early before Hannah and his mother were up, and on a tip from the barman at the saloon in Chico, they rode east toward the Sierra Nevada Mountains taking the road most travelled.

At a small store along the trail called Paradise Inn, they described Polk to the store keeper as 'a man with burns on one side of his face'. No, he said, he hadn't seen anyone of that description in the last few weeks.

They rode on east toward Quincy's Station, a single store in a flat spot higher in the mountains where they began to see a few prospectors walking along beside overloaded mules. A card game was in progress in the rear of the store and Bill described Polk again.

'Yeah, I know old Polk. He was in here playing about three weeks ago, played a few hands and left like someone was trailin' him. Said he was headin' for Reno to find some card action. He looked kinda nervous like maybe he was on the run. I know that look; seen it before. I try to steer clear of fellas like Jed Polk. He's bad medicine. Tempermental sort and too ready to use his gun. If you're huntin' him, he could be anywhere's by now, but Reno was where he said he was headin' when he was here.'

'Much obliged for the information,' said Bill. 'Bartender, give these gentlemen a drink on us.' And Bill placed a silver dollar on the counter on the way out.

Outside they discussed their plans.

'Well, Finn we've covered about eighty miles so far and it's another eighty to Reno, so I reckon we should find a good spot and make camp. What say?'

'That sounds good to me. I'm about worn out from this saddle and could stand some of that chow we've been carrying'.'

Three miles later they had to cross a wide river; the river was fairly shallow at both sides, but deep in the center and Bill knew they would have to swim their horses and the mule. Mules were always reluctant to enter water, so Bill warned Finn about him.

'We may oughta offload some of our gear from the mule and take it across on our horses. It wouldn't hurt to make several trips to get er done.

'Think your horse is a swimmer, Finn?'

Finn spurred his horse down the bank and into the shallow water.

'Guess we'll find out pretty quick, Bill.'

He rode his horse toward the other side until his horse slid off into the deep water. Luckily, Finn's horse was a fine swimmer, and in no time his horse climbed the bank at the other side where Finn stowed some of the gear taken from the mule.

Bill Mackey's horse was almost as good, but once in the deeper water the horse began to drift downstream, and Bill turned him with the reins; the horse eventually made the far shore and up the bank.

'Musta been the extra load I was carryin'. He's usually a good swimmer.'

Two more trips and they had all the gear across. Then they went back and each put a rope on the mule and led him into the shallow water. He balked when he came to the drop off, but with both riders pulling on him, he finally submitted and swam across without incident. They loaded the gear back on the mule and continued their journey.

They rode about seven more miles up steep trails and were finally close to the peak of the mountains. The winds whipped up, and Bill found a nice snug place under a rock ledge to pitch their camp. Nearby were the remains of an old mining shack which had been torn apart over time for firewood. Finn hobbled the horses and their mule, unloaded and fed them oats in a feed bag since there was not much natural forage at this point. Bill gathered firewood from the floor of the old shack.

'Saw some smoke a while back, Finn. Best keep that Colt ready just in case. There's injuns in this part of the mountains and I don't know if they're friendly or not. Let's get an early start tomorrow. I've made a small dry-wood fire and coffee is brewing. Be ready in a few minutes.'

They ate their food in silence and Bill cleaned his shotgun while Finn rested near the fire. Inwardly, Finn was thanking Bill for convincing him to buy good quality gear. He could see how life could be miserable on the trail if he had second rate equipment.

Early the next morning Finn woke to the sound of fire crackling, and looked up to see Bill hoisting a small frying pan.

'Breakfast in a minute, Finn. The mule is packed and ready. We'd best be on our way after breakfast. I have an uneasy feeling about this place. I know it sounds queer, but I smell Indians, so let's move out quick.'

An hour later Bill called a halt.

'Keep your eyes open, Finn. I saw two Indians trailin' us the last fifteen minutes.'

Finn glanced around him at the rocky walls and huge boulders near the trail.

'This'd be a great place for an ambush,' he said as he checked his gun again and followed as Bill kicked his horse into a trot while pulling on the mule's halter.

At the top of a rise ahead of them stood three Indians, two with old muzzle-loaders. The other one had a bow and a quiver of arrows. They sat still watching the two riders climb the steep trail. Bill glanced all around looking for more Indians but saw none.

'Look like Paiutes to me, Finn. They can be hellacious fighters if they're a mind to, so keep that gun free and handy.'

He adjusted his shotgun and told Finn to be on the lookout. In a few minutes two more Indians showed up barring their path.

The lead Indian had an old musket-loading rifle as did one other one in the rear; the rest had bows and steel-tipped arrows. The lead man with a rifle rode his pony up nose-to-nose with Blue who snorted and shied away from the Indian pony.

'This Paiute Indian lands. You pay ta-riff. Horses and side-arm pistols. You pay now. Then you go in peace.'

The Indian pointed his rifle at Finn, and fearing for his life, Finn fast-drew his pistol and shot the Indian in the head, and the Indian dropped his rifle in the dirt. The second muzzle-loader fired at Finn, but nicked the front brim of his hat, and Bill Mackey killed that Indian with his shotgun.

The three remaining Indians hopped off their ponies and raised dust as they dove behind the rocks. Bill and Finn quickly led their horses and pack mule into a cluster of huge boulders.

'Finn, I think two of these last three have bows and arrows, the other one has an old muzzle-loader. Never can tell how good a shot he might be. Use caution, Finn. These redskins mean business. From the looks of their gear, they want our guns and ammo and anything else they can get, which mean they'll kill us to get our gear unless we kill them first.'

'Okay, Bill. I used one shot on that first Indian so I have four shots left, and I have an extra cylinder loaded plus my rifle.'

Finn crouched behind the lowest rock and sighted where he had last seen the Indians. He saw a slight movement across the trail, but waited till he could get a better shot. Bill Mackey heard the twang.

'Duck, Finn. They're shootin' arrows.'

They lay low clinging tight to the rocks as arrows came over their heads and glanced off the rocks behind them.

Suddenly one Indian with a knife charged across between two boulders, trying to draw their fire, but Finn couldn't get off a shot, and Bill stayed put ready for anything.

An Indian rushed from one rock toward another, and Finn sighted and shot him before he could get to cover. The Indian fell and somersaulted, screaming loudly as he fell. There were two Indians left, and Finn heard their ponies riding off. Finn jumped out from behind the rocks, saw the two Indians, and shot the one in the rear who tumbled from his pony and fell to the ground dead. The last one grabbed the rope on his friend's horse and led him off into the boulders, riding low against his horse's back, making a difficult target. Both men took shots at the fleeing Indian but he kept riding hard and suddenly charged from the maze of rocks onto a flat plain.

'Git your rifle, Finn. Maybe you can get a shot at him.'

Finn dashed to his horse, pulled the Kentucky rifle from the scabbard and ran out in the open. He sighted on the Indian who ran across Finn's field of vision. Thinking he was well out of range of their guns, the Indian turned on a direct course away from Finn, and Finn locked in his target just like he did back at the orchards. He fired and watched the Indian as his pony galloped away. Suddenly he lay flat against the pony's neck and finally fell off.

'Wow! What a shot, Finn. I think we're free of injuns for now,' he said as he walked toward the dead Indian, taking precise steps and mumbling to himself.

'Bill, what are you doing?'

'Counting. Don't bother me.'

Finn watched him as he walked to the Indian lying on the ground. Bill turned and ran back to his horse.

Finn and Bill now found themselves with three Indian ponies, two old musket rifles, and two bows and quivers of arrows. They scattered the ponies, and broke the bows, arrows, and rifles, and bent the barrels.

'Let's not take any chances, Finn. There may be more of their friends nearby.'

'Bill, what were you doing out there?'

'Counting. You jist shot that injun off his pony at two-hundred, seventy yards. By dam, what a shot,' he said as he spurred his horse forward with the mule's rope in his hand.

They continued on their way through the mountains toward Reno, rapidly putting distance between themselves and any more Indians.

Chapter 21

January 1, 1848

As they rode into Reno on January 1, 1848, Bill Mackey looked for a livery stable.

'Our horses are spent, Finn. We need to get some food and water into 'em and give 'em a rest.'

Once the horses were taken care of, Bill looked up the sheriff, found he knew the man, Norman Croft, and told them who they were looking for. One deputy was familiar with Polk, and said that he'd seen him at the Sagebrush Saloon playing cards several times lately. Finn asked the deputy for directions to the Saloon, while Bill tried to enlist the help of Sheriff Croft and his deputies in capturing Polk for the murder of Finn's father in the Maidu camp. Before Bill could say anything, Finn walked quickly away from the sheriff's office heading for the Sagebrush Saloon.

'Finn, wait. Let's get some help from the sheriff...Finn,' he yelled, but Finn had turned a corner and disappeared.

'Dam fool young'un,' he said to Croft. 'He's liable to get his self shot by Polk. Can you send some deputies over to the Sagebrush with me?'

Mackey, during his training sessions with Finn, always confided that the best way to kill an adversary was to shoot him in an unexpected fashion before he had time to draw his gun, because giving the other fella an even chance was too risky. But Finn's limited knowledge of the western code of honor had convinced him that a one-on-one duel was the proper way to confront Polk, and that's what he had decided to do. Bill Mackey was certain that Jed Polk had no such qualms about shooting anyone.

Finn pushed through the swinging doors of the bar, stood still till his eyes adjusted to the dim light, and headed for the bartender.

'Hey, partner, I'm looking for Jed Polk. I hear he plays cards here on occasion. Is he around today?'

The bartender wiped a glass and studied Finn for a moment.

'Yeah. There's a card game in the back room. Go through that door over there.'

'Thanks. Guess I'll surprise him,' he said with a smile.

He walked to the door which was partly open, pushed it open all the way, and stood for a moment sizing up the small room. He saw a round poker table with six players and studied each one as he walked quietly around the table, until he realized which one was Polk. In the light over the table, he could see the shriveled darkened skin above the beard. None of the other players had burns on their faces, not like Polk's. One side of his face was burned, and he no longer had an eyebrow on that side.

Finn stood facing Polk across the table.

'Are you Jed Polk?'

Polk instantly lowered his cards, placed them on the table, and looked up at Finn, a slim young greenhorn who he'd never seen before. He pushed his chair back a foot and sat up, his hands below the edge of the table.

'Yeah, I'm Polk. Who wants to know?'

'I'm Finn Kerry. You shot and killed my father, Sean Kerry, near the Maidu village where you and Jasper Biggs were trying to rape a young Indian girl, and I'm calling you out as a dirty no-good skunk who shot an unarmed man…'

Three of the players jumped to their feet, their eyes on Polk who looked like he was about to draw his pistol. Before he could clear the holster, the player next to him grabbed his arm and twisted it behind his back.

'No gun play in here, Polk. Take your argument outside. I had you pegged for a crook right from the start. I've had enough of you and your cheatin' ways, Polk. Is this fella telling the truth? You shot an unarmed man? And you tried to rape a young girl?' He looked over at Finn. 'You say he shot your pa? And he wasn't armed?'

'That's right, my dad is…was an orchardist and never carried a gun. I have several witnesses who saw the whole thing, and his buddy, Biggs, was killed trying to escape the Indians.'

'That's a damned lie. I don't know what he's talking about.'

'You're a lying killer, Polk, and I'm calling you out to a gunfight, just the two of us – if you have the guts.'

Finn had called Polk out in front of his gambling friends, and after Polk sized up the tall, thin young man, decided he could take him, even in a shootout, if necessary.

'He was riding me down with his horse. I had to protect myself.'

'Not by shooting an unarmed man, you didn't,' yelled the man holding Polk's arm.

The others agreed, and two men held Polk's arms while they forced him out the door into the main bar room. One of the men holding Polk's arms turned to Finn as they hustled Polk toward the front door.

'You sure you wanna give this bastard an even break? You could kill him now and nobody'd blame you. The sheriff would understand.'

Finn shook his head.

'No I want to see his face when I kill him.'

Polk laughed. 'In your dreams, *sonny*.'

Let's go outside, Polk,' said Finn as he headed for the entrance, 'and see who's dreaming.'

The men sitting at the tables rose and watched the procession heading for the front door.

'What's going on?' asked one of the men.

'Polk shot an unarmed man while trying to rape a young girl. This fella here claims he shot and killed his pa, and he wants satisfaction. He's challenged Polk to a shootout out front.'

The word spread quickly around the bar patrons. Polk was being forced toward the door and most of the Sagebrush patrons followed, eager to see a real gunfight. Polk watched for an opportunity to gun Finn down before a real duel took place, but with the men holding him and the crowd on his heels, he had no chance to get to his gun.

They moved to the center of the street in front of the saloon, and Finn walked quickly to a location with the sun at his back.

The two men were about thirty feet apart, arranged by Finn as he backed away from Polk. Polk stood head-on facing Finn with his pistol in

126

a holster on his right side. He took off his coat to free his hands and arms and laid it over a hitching post, and then walked to the center of the street. You could see the confidence growing in him now that the contest had been decided. He knew he could take this thin young man.

Finn turned so that his left side faced Polk, making him a slim target. Polk was a bit nervous at this stance as he had never been in a true duel with another man in his life, and he worried a bit about this thin target. All his gun play had been done while drawing and firing at an opponent five or six feet away sitting at a card table, or as Polk liked to do it, dry-gulching a man in an alley or in front of a lighted window with Polk looking at the man silhouetted in the light.

Both gun fighters had the same model gun, the Colt Baby Dragoon with a .31 caliber ball and cap. Finn had been trained in dueling—on how to draw, cock, raise his arm, sight, and slow-squeeze the trigger while making a paper-thin target of himself with the sun behind him. Polk's gun-fighting experience was mostly head-to-head in card games where his fast draw always saved the day, and he had a close unprepared target. He seldom used the sights on his pistol.

The crowd filled the wooden sidewalks or stood on level ground behind horses tied to the hitching posts, but definitely out of the path of the two gun fighters. A few women had stepped out of local stores when they saw the crowd gathering. Many of the saloon patrons carried their drinks with them onto the covered porch and onto the street near horses or other cover. Several gamblers were making bets on the winner and a few of the saloon patrons joined in.

'My money's on Polk,' said one man, but the man next to him said, 'Wal, my poke is on the skinny kid. He looks like he means business.'

Finn tied the leather thong around his left leg below the holster, took several deep breaths, relaxed, and flapped his arms and hands to loosen his muscles as Mackey had taught him. For the first time, he could feel his pulse quicken. As the duel was about to take place, Finn realized that he had never faced a man like this before.

Polk watched Finn's actions, and he began to shake his arms, too.

Bill Mackey and two deputies walked up as the two men were setting themselves. Bill looked at Finn.

'Finn, you sure you want to do this?'

Finn looked over at Bill and nodded.

'Yes, I'm sure,' Finn said as he eyed Polk standing ready in the street, making a good target.

Bill appealed to the deputies.

'You gonna stop this here duel, deputy?'

One of the deputies laughed.

'Heck no. Never seen no one-on-one gun fight before. All seems fair and square to me. How about you Buck?'

'You bet. Let 'er rip!'

Finn looked over the crowd, saw the badge on the deputy standing by a horse about midway between him and Polk, and saw Bill Mackey standing next to the two deputies, their shiny badges flashing in the sunlight. He could feel the drumming of his heart now that the shootout was about to happen.

'Would one of you deputies count to three for us in a loud voice?' He asked as he glanced at Polk who was setting himself with his weight balanced on both feet.

Hank, one of the two deputies stepped forward.

'Sure, I'll do 'er. Jist count to three, is that all?'

Finn nodded. 'Yes, thank you.' He glanced at Polk. 'You ready to go to hell, you murdering bastard?'

Polk looked at Finn and laughed nervously.

'I guess we'll see who goes to hell, *sonny*. You're gonna come to a rude ending in a few moments, so say your prayers, kid.'

The shuffling quieted and all eyes were on one or the other of the gun fighters or on the deputy counting. Finn felt totally relaxed now, although facing another man was a new experience for him. All he had to do was remember what Bill Mackey had taught him. His actions with his pistol were almost a ritual by now. He turned sideways so that his left side was toward Polk. He placed his right hand on his hip and was calm.

'Okay. Are you both ready? I'm gonna start counting now.'

Both men nodded while they watched each other closely.

'One—two—three...'

Polk's gun rose to his waist from his holster in a blinding flash, he cocked the hammer as he raised his gun waist-high, and fired. There was no way he could have aimed and squeezed the trigger like Finn had been taught. As Bill had described it to Finn, the man was pointing and shooting, not truly aiming. Polk kept his arm belt-high, fanned the hammer, and fired again. He fanned the hammer again, ready for a third shot.

Meanwhile at the count of 'three', Finn's gun rose from his holster in a smooth liquid motion, the hammer cocked almost before the gun cleared the holster. He sighted as he had done many times before, and slowly let out his breath. As he squeezed the trigger, he felt a stab in his right sleeve and reflexively moved his right arm further behind him, and then, just as he fired, his hat brim on the left side flipped up slightly.

The air around both gun fighters filled with smoke from the powder explosions, and Finn cocked his pistol again, aimed, ready to squeeze the trigger a second time.

As the smoke cleared, he saw Polk drop to one knee, his gun half-raised, and Finn could see him straining to pull the trigger again. Blood ran down his nose and into his glazed eyes as he looked at Finn in disbelief. With a twist his leg collapsed, Polk fell and landed on his back, his hand trying to raise the gun again, and then his arm dropped into the dust and he lay still.

The crowd surged forward, surrounding both gunmen. Someone knelt next to Polk and examined him for wounds, but there was no doubt.

'Shot right in the middle of the forehead. Man, what a shot!' He turned toward Finn. 'From thirty or more feet away, too. Man, that's shootin'. And with one shot, too.'

The shuffle of feet was hardly heard by Finn who stood in a daze while well-wishers clapped him on the back and shouted words of praise for his feat. He put his left hand on his right arm above the elbow and realized he was shot. He looked down at his arm and saw blood on his sleeve, and as he dropped his arm, blood ran down his hand and dripped onto the dusty street.

Near the saloon porch, money changed hands as bets were paid off.

'Hey, Wally, look at him. He looks like a kid,' said a bald man with a large belly. He turned to the man next to him. 'Did you see that cool calm draw? He actually *squeezed* that there trigger. Never saw anythin' like it before. He must be a perfesh'nal, and for a young gun slinger, he must have nerves of steel, standin' and squeezin' the trigger like that while the other guy got off two shots at him.'

Doctor Hanes made his way from his office across the street to where Finn stood with men all around him.

'You okay? I'm Dr. Hanes. I saw the whole thing from my office window.'

Finn looked around at the man as if in a dream. He raised his right arm mechanically and showed the doctor his arm.

'Guess he got me in the arm, doc. And I think he may have ruined my hat, too.'

The crowd laughed at his comment, and Dr. Hanes tended to his arm.

'Did'ja hear that, Ed? The kid's worried about his ruint hat. Don't that beat all?'

Several men nearby laughed.

'You were lucky, son,' said Dr. Hanes. 'It's just a flesh wound. Ball went in and out in the fleshy part of your upper arm. Come on over to my office and I'll disinfect and bandage it for you. No charge.'

Finn followed the doctor instinctively and climbed the stairs on the side of the building while several men stood below watching. Finn's stomach began to churn, and his legs began to feel weak, like he'd been in a long fist fight.

Bill Mackey talked to his friend, Sheriff Croft, and tried to convince him that the killing of Polk was justice for the killing of Finn's father, Sean Kerry. The sheriff agreed, but said he had to wait for a visit from the district judge in order to legally clear Finn of any charges.

So after Dr. Hanes bandaged his arm, Finn was led to the Reno jail, and spent the next week waiting for the circuit judge. Dr. Hanes visited him every other day, and they played checkers. Finally when the judge hadn't arrived, Sheriff Croft freed Finn and told him to stay in town till the judge arrived.

Bill and Finn made the rounds of the better bars and got free drinks from contented gamblers who had known Polk as a nasty character or had lost money to him.

Chapter 22

January 1848

On January, 30, 1848 while Finn waited for the judge, he heard the news of two gold strikes, one near Coloma, California on January 28, where gold nuggets had been found by a carpenter, James Marshall, while he was building a saw mill for Captain Sutter, and another strike at nearly the same time in the north near the Oregon border on the Yuba River. Finn knew that the Kerry Orchards, located between both strike areas, would soon be overrun with prospectors searching for gold.

Then Finn got the news that John Bidwell had discovered gold at Bidwell Bar on the Feather River, and he knew that he must get home quickly. He figured that if prospectors were flocking to the Feather River, then they would soon be on Deer Creek up in the mountains, and that was too close to his orchards for comfort.

The judge finally arrived, talked to the sheriff, and dismissed all charges against Finn Kerry in the shooting death of Jed Polk. According to the judge, 'Justice had been served.'

Finn knew that his father had found his first gold nuggets in October 1847, and by November 1847 had accumulated a small fortune, most of it before Finn had arrived at the Kerry Orchards; however, Sean Kerry was not interested in gold, since he had his orchards and plenty of the work he loved to keep him busy. But he was smart enough to realize that he must hide what he had for the time being. The trouble was he was shot and killed before he told Finn or his mother where he had hid the gold. Maybe the Maidu Indian boys would know about Sean's gold, he thought. I must talk to them when I get home. And on the outside chance that his father had put the money in the Chico bank, he would talk to Banker Stillman, too.

'Bill, it's time to be gettin' home. I have a feeling my family may have trouble with gold prospectors, and they're going to need me. They'll be all over the Sierra Nevada Mountains now, and our place is right in the middle of those mountains.'

They made the perilous 163-mile journey through the mountains from Reno to the Kerry Orchards during February 1848 and arrived at the Kerry Orchards on the first of March, half-frozen, worn, and tired. They had lost their pack mule on an icy ledge when the mule slipped and fell over a seventy-five-foot cliff with all their gear.

Their homecoming was hailed by hugs from his mother and his wife, Hannah.

As Hannah hugged him, she said, 'Oh Finn, I was so worried. Bill said you were cool as could be and killed that man, Polk, with one shot. I'm so proud of you.' She noticed his right arm was in a sling.

'Finn, you've been wounded.'

He smiled.

'I'm okay, Hannah. Guess I got in the best shot because here I am.'

Jennifer prepared a big meal, and Bill Mackey couldn't refuse. They sat on the porch for a while after dinner and enjoyed the leisure even though it was chilly. Finally Bill rose, said his goodbyes to the ladies, and turned to Finn.

'Well, Finn I reckon I'll ride on into Chico and check my gun sales. It's been a pleasure partnerin' with you. I 'spect we'll be runnin' into each other from time to time...' He turned toward Jennifer. 'Ma'am I'm right pleased to have met you, and I sure did enjoy your cookin'. He turned to Hannah. 'And that goes for you, too, little lady.' He touched the brim of his hat.

'And if you ever feel the need for male companionship, you can count on me,' he said with a smile and a wink toward Jennifer.

Jennifer laughed and waved.

Finn walked to Bill's horse and touched his arm.

'Bill, I've wanted to say something to you for a few days now. It's been nagging at me all the way home.

'I didn't have any trouble killing those Indians since they were after our lives and we did what we had to do. But Jed Polk was another story. Maybe I did wrong going out after the man the way I did. I'll always feel like I made a mistake with Polk, even though he fired the shot that killed my Dad. When he fell, I felt vindicated in what I did. Does that make any sense?'

Bill studied Finn for a minute and shook his head.

'Wal, knowin' you the way I do, I'd be a might surprised if you didn't have second thoughts about what you did in Reno. In my mind you were justified in killing Polk, and unlike many men I've known, you gave the man an even chance and that's sayin' a lot about you. I take off my hat to you the way you handled the whole affair. If I was you, I'd forget the whole thing and jist git on with yer life with that new wife of yers.'

He took Finn by the shoulder.

'You know, Finn, you have a reputation now as a shootist. Men figure you're a professional gunslinger. Why I heard some men talkin' about runnin' you for sheriff.'

And with that Bill walked his horse away from the water trough, slung his saddle bags full of weapons and ammunition behind his saddle, mounted the horse, tipped his hat to Finn, and said, 'You take care now, hear?' and rode off in the direction of Chico. Finn watched him ride down the trail until Bill was out of sight.

Just as Finn had figured, Hannah and his mother had already been plagued by prospectors looking for food, and there had been two break-ins with tools stolen from the shop. Hannah thought she may have wounded one man with the rifle as he was sneaking out of the shed. She found blood on the ground the next morning.

Two of their fences were broken and cut, and several tree limbs were broken where men had climbed into trees looking for fruit. Luckily, the harvests were over and there was little fruit to be had. The apples were still too green for eating, and would give the eater a terrible stomach ache.

From that day on, Finn kept all guns loaded and ready to defend their home and property. As fast as he could, he put up 'No Trespassing' signs along his orchard fences.

* * *

By August seven months had passed; Finn had seen ragged men with their mules or carts full of rattling equipment like pans and shovels and rough tools as they filed past his orchards on their way to gold claims somewhere along Deer Creek, although he had heard that many men also wended their way into the nearby mountains and panned for gold along the Feather River and creeks running into it. Other times he saw small groups of men on mules heading *toward* Chico with nothing more than their bags of gold dust. They came and went at all times of the day and night, usually in small groups of four or five. There's safety in numbers, Finn thought.

He watched them from a ladder, and could hear them cussing at their mules or their dogs or at each other as they plodded along the already well-worn path.

After weeks of this, Finn's curiosity got the best of him, and he decided the time was right to discover where these men worked gold claims. So late one morning, Finn filled a canteen, loaded his Colt, stuffed jerky into his coat pocket, picked the choicest fruits from the fruit storage boxes, filled a bag, hung the it over his saddle horn, and turned Blue out onto the path.

He followed the winding trail until he came out at Deer Creek where the path continued east along the edge for about a mile, and there he discovered an offshoot creek flowing into Deer Creek, and the path forked, turned up beside this smaller creek, and on up along Deer Creek, too.

He rode up this fork for about five minutes and finally saw smoke ahead. He rode Blue near the water until he saw men working over the creek. Panning for gold, he thought, and kept Blue moving till he reached the first man.

The view ahead surprised him, for he'd never actually seen men panning for gold before. Strung out all along the creek were men every 20 or 30 feet coming and going from the water, swishing pans, picking bits of gold from the sand in their pans, or emptying the pan contents into little leather bags. He took a quick count and figured there were at least 25 men in this portion of the creek alone. He saw mules standing along the banks behind the working men, some with bedrolls behind dirty saddles, and in some places small wooden shacks built into the hillside or hammocks strung between available trees.

As he reached the first kneeling man, he pulled Blue to a halt. The man looked up at him in surprise, and immediately grabbed the rifle resting on an old stump, and held it across his chest.

Finn looked over the working men; filthy dirty, their clothes in rags, two and three-week-old beards, some full of tobacco juice stains, torn trousers, and in some cases, no trousers or shirts at all, filthy-looking slouchy, limp-looking hats with wide brims turned down to keep off the sun, or a few with old army caps with wide front bills, most of the men with small leather bags or pouches hanging from their belts. He laughed to himself. Within feet of clean water, and they're filthy as pigs, he thought. Now that's concentration.

On the side of the hill were a number of one- and two-man tents and in front of most a cooking pot hung on a tripod of wood. By one camp, Finn saw a banjo resting against a tree, and several mongrel dogs on chains near claims. He looked up and noticed men brandishing pistols and rifles.

'You want somethin', mister?'

Finn scrutinized the men as they squinted at him and held up his hands in surrender.

'Howdy, fellas. I come in peace. Having any luck?'

He reached into his fruit bag for an apple and heard the cocking of five or more pistols and rifles.

The burley giant in front of him with no shirt, grunted, raised his rifle toward Finn and rose from the water's edge.

'Stranger, you don't come on gold-seekers and ask a fool question like thet. And you sure as heck don't reach into bags without warnin' us before hand. Where'd you come from, anyways?'

Finn looked down at the big man and unhooked his fruit bag from the saddle.

'Care for a piece of fresh fruit, partner?' he asked and held out the bag.

The man stood looking at him as if he were crazy, and eyed Finn's bag with suspicion.

Finn took a bite out of his apple, the crunch sounding loud and sharp in the sudden quiet of the grove. All he could hear was the gentle tinkle of water across rocks in the creek. The men were all standing as if in suspended animation, their eyes on Finn and his bulging bag.

The big man turned and yelled up to his friends.

'Hey Burnsey, this fella's got a bag of fruit, and it looks fresh, too.'

In moments Finn was surrounded by men with dripping boots or bare-foot as they crowded around his horse, and all the men were eyeing his fruit bag. Finn looked them over in dismay.

'I'm sorry, gents, but I don't have enough fruit for all of you.' Then he thought quickly. 'But I can bring you more another day from my orchards.'

'How much?' Someone yelled from upstream.

Finn thought a moment.

'Well, I'd charge you just what they'd charge you in Chico, but I might have to throw in another two-bits if I have to deliver them here.'

'Last time I was in Chico, they charged me $2 fer a pear, and that was discounted 'cause it wasn't too fresh. Is that what you charge, mister?'

Finn looked at the man in surprise.

'$2 for a pear? Who'd you buy it from?'

'Carter's up beyond the general store. Simms was out of fruit last time I was there.'

Finn puzzled over this. Carter's was one of his customers and Finn sold him fruit at 10 cents per apple.

'You sure about that price?'

'Dam sure, mister. And they don't last long either. They could probly get more if they were a mind to and if they had more fruit. We don't get into town often and we usually have to take what they have to offer. We all need fruit to keep scurvy away, and it keeps us healthy.'

Finn had read about scurvy, a lack of vitamin C found in ascorbic acid, present in fruits and vegetables. The results of scurvy were not pleasant. First, gums became red and soft, teeth grew loose, and later as the disease advanced, open suppurating wounds could be seen, and men lost their teeth, sometimes had jaundice, and in the end could die if not treated properly.

Finn realized that Carter's—and maybe other merchants—were selling his fruit way beyond what Finn was charging them. A profit's a profit, he thought, but this was ridiculous. He was being robbed by the very merchants he sold to. He tried to puzzle out what he should do.

'Look, I own the Kerry Orchards. My name is Finn Kerry, and...'

There was a buzz of talk along the creek, and some men were pointing at Finn and saying his name.

The big man by his leg looked up and lowered his rifle.

'You the Kerry what shot Jed Polk?'

Finn made a wry face, nodded and shrugged. 'Yep, afraid that's me.'

The man turned and yelled.

'Hey, fellas, we got us a real live professional gunman in our mist.'

The men were crowding in on Finn.

'How much for one of them apples, Mr. Kerry?'

'I work with the Chico merchants and sell them apples, apricots, plums and pears. If I bring fruit to you here, I might consider a higher charge, and I'd have to throw in my travel time.

'I could probably bring four bushels by mule if you're interested.'

'How often?'

'Well, every two weeks while the fruits are in season...'

'Where's your place Mr. Kerry? Could I ride over there to pick some up?'

'Yes. In fact, on Saturdays I open one orchard so folks can pick their own.'

He gave them directions to the Kerry Orchards.

The big man said, 'I think $2 an apple is worth every penny for fresh fruit, don't you, boys? And Mister Kerry says he'll deliver it to us here. It would sure guarantee against scurvy. That's what Tim McFee died of last month.'

Amid the yelling, the consensus was 'yes', and Finn Kerry suddenly found himself with potential profits beyond his wildest dreams. Most men paid him for the fruit he had with pure gold dust at one-tenth ounce per apple and pear, and one-twentieth ounce per apricot and plum, but the men were eager for the fruit and most overpaid him.

Several of the men offered to share their lunch with Finn, and he finally accepted the big man's offer, not eager to get home to his orchards this afternoon. He had found a bonanza and wanted to get to know these men.

Finn dismounted and tied his horse to a small tree.

'Names Carl Banks,' the big man said and shook Finn's hand. 'Have a venison stew if you don't mind eatin' off of a tin plate. Was lucky and got a deer few days back, otherwise, all I could offer you is beans and bacon.'

Finn nodded and took the proffered plate, sat down by the fire Carl had going, and held out the plate as Carl filled it with savory-smelling stew.

Carl grinned at him.

'So yer the gent what did in Jed Polk. Lost some gold dust to him one night in a card game in Chico. Allays did think the skunk was cheatin', and so did others, but nobody could catch him at it. And he had a reputation as a gunman, so nobody wanted to argue with him. He allays had that slick charm about him, too, probly tryin' to make up for that ugly face of his. Right glad he got his come-uppance; hated starin' at him across the table all evenin'. How's the stew Mr. Kerry?'

'Call me Finn. And the stew is great. One of my favorites. So, Carl, where are you from?'

'Pennsylvania. Was a carpenter there. Left a wife and four little ones waitin' till I get back with a lot of money. Huh! They don't know the half of it. Got here too late to get a choice claim, but this creek produces fairly well; about twenty ounces a week. That's about $400 in cash money. Six months ago, fellas was makin' $2000 a week outa this here creek, but the gold is getting' scarce. At first I figured in six months I could clear nearly $10,000 and walk away from here a rich man, but I never figured on the cost of livin'. That's takin' half my weeks findin's. Now we have to worry about scurvy, so we need more vegetables and fruit. Had two miners died last month because of scurvy. We really need that fruit, Mr. Kerry.'

Lunch finished, Finn said his 'goodbyes' and mounted Blue.

He yelled to those busy along the creek.

'Be back in a few days with four bushels of fresh fruit. Have a good day, gents.'

As he rode away from the creek, he waved, and heard several shouts in response.

* * *

Over the next months, Finn scoured the creeks and streams of Deer Creek up into the mountains, and the Feather River and its creeks looking for more groups of hungry men eager for fresh fruit, and soon he had a brand new business venture which was making him more money than all of the merchants in Chico combined. After he realized what the merchants were charging, he increased his prices to merchants to almost half of what they were selling the fruit for. They were unhappy, but accepted his increase.

He found he could cater to up to four groups of men like those on the first stream on Deer Creek without impacting his normal business, but deliveries seriously ate into his days, and he missed working in the orchards with the Indian boys.

His mule could easily carry 4 bushels of fruit, and Finn tried to have at least one bushel of each of his fruits on every trip depending on the season, and made two trips per month to each camp.

His delivery menu was as follows:

Apples — 120/bushel	@ $2 each	$240/bu
Pears — 120/bushel	@ $2 each	$240/bu
Plums — 240/bushel	@ $1 each	$240/bu
Apricots — 240/bushel	@ $1 each	$240/bu
Plus travel time		$ 40
Total per trip		$1000
Profit per trip to 4 groups		$4000
Total profit per month for 2 trips to each		$8000

Therefore, without much of a struggle, Finn was able to bank roughly $8000 per month. In one sense, he felt guilty taking $240 per bushel, but these men were crying for fresh fruit because of the dangers of scurvy, and the Chico stores had taken advantage of them. Now because the men felt that $2 per apple seemed fair to them, he too was making huge profits from their needs. He was certain that the fruits he was selling directly to the prospectors wouldn't even make a dent in the profits being enjoyed by the Chico merchants. And he felt that his trips twice a month to these disheveled men helped keep them healthy, and maybe even saved their lives.

139

Hannah and his mother were amazed at his business acumen.

He smiled proudly and said, 'Simply a matter of going up the right streams, ladies.'

Finn suggested that the women prepare bags of vegetables from their garden that he could take to these men. The women agreed, and had a small profit from their gardening to make up for all their work.

Chapter 23

September 1848

All through September, Finn studied his father's notes and the books he had on plants. He had also accumulated several recent books while at Hanford Publishing and spent an hour or more every day poring over them, looking for hints on how to improve the Kerry fruits.

The experimental orchard in the rear of the house was taking on new meaning since Finn had taken over the orchards. He was trying new strains of apples and apricots and pears, hoping to improve the quality of their output over time.

He had found two of the Indian boys who were interested in fruit growing and plant-growing in general; Ruma, Chief Sam's son, and Ipsa. Both boys were constantly asking Finn questions about planting methods, and with Finn's help, they had started a small orchard near the Maidu village.

Finn had helped the boys obtain the tools necessary to maintain their orchard, and they were always eager to venture into any new project that Finn wanted to try.

The Indians began to borrow Finn's plant catalogs and learned more and more about growing fruits and other vegetables, and in the process improved their English. As expected, Finn was deluged with questions as the Indians learned more and more about agriculture. Still the Maidu adult men refused to take part in the new growing trend for they were still hunters.

And now with the gold rush in full swing, he found his fruit business increasing; everyone in and around Chico wanted fresh produce and especially fruit, so Finn was making more trips with his fruit cargos and getting better prices, too. He had picked up several new customers in Chico to whom he could sell his fruits, and the Kerry income was increasing every month. These expansions had happened almost overnight. He had indicated to the Chico merchants that he knew the prices they were receiving for his fruits, and suggested pointedly that they share that profit with Finn. He was now making almost fifty cents per apple and pear, and twenty-five cents per plum and apricot from the merchants.

During the gold rush some of the stores in Chico were so eager to get his fruits that they sent their own wagons to bring back loads of fruit.

* * *

On every trip into Chico, Finn was amazed at the changes taking place. New buildings were going up almost overnight, and gold prospectors had established a tent-city beyond the boundaries of Chico's town limits. Sheriff Clayton had hired three new deputies who were now constantly patrolling the streets of the city. New signs were posted on all incoming roads warning visitors to check their guns with the Sheriff's office.

Even with these measures, the town was bustling with prospectors, gamblers, con men, thieves, and a raft of new business ventures, all attempting to take advantage of the influx of gold. Everywhere gold scales were in evidence.

During the gold rush, gold was used for purchases of food, lodgings, and entertainment, mostly in the form of gold dust which was weighed on gold scales on the spot in all mining towns like Chico and Coloma.

It was carefully weighed out by merchants and vendors who used the gold traded or bartered to buy supplies from middlemen who bought from ship captains or packers bringing goods into California by ship or mule train.

The fortunate gold prospectors took their gold home.

Others sent it home.

Local banks and gold dealers began to issue 'bank notes' or 'drafts'; this was locally accepted currency so prospectors didn't have to carry their gold around with them.

Private mints created gold coins.

Finn's business escalated quickly after gold was discovered, but with the increased market for his fruits, also came new dangers in the form of thievery and occasional vandalism. Luckily, his weapons training with Mackey paid off, and he easily protected his family from danger.

In general, Finn's fruits drew more folks to his orchards, and at times he allowed visitors to pick their own fruit in certain parts of his orchards – at a price, of course. As the gold rush moved forward, he began to see more and more of the gold prospectors. The town of Chico and other small towns along the Sacramento River to the south wanted to hire him as their sheriff, but at the moment Finn was too much absorbed with his orchards and marketing, and law enforcement was not in his scheme of things except perhaps as a part-time deputy, but right now he didn't need that kind of money, although the sheriff asked him every few weeks.

Wildlife occasionally tore down Finn's fences circling the orchards, so he always had fence repairs to make, and the Indian boys helped him with this. Deer would usually eat the leaves off of young trees, and fruit off older ones. He also knew that he had to protect his hay storage from the deer, so any hay he had on hand stayed in the loft till needed.

He had several strategies to protect against deer: First, let the Indians kill any deer near his property; second, hang bars of soap or tufts of long hair at the periphery of his orchards, or hang multiple cans at the periphery which made noise when the cans clashed.

During the gold rush days he was plagued with vandalism and was forced to shoot warning shots several times to scare off thieves. Soon his reputation as a gun man circulated around the Sierra Nevada Mountains, and marauders bothered his property less and less.

In the year after the death of his father, Jennifer suggested Finn go through his father's things and see if there was anything he wanted to keep, for she was getting ready to sell things and give some away.

Finn rummaged through Sean's possessions; Sean's trunks were a treasure trove of books on botany and plant life, old coins, clocks, worn-out plant scales, mirrors, old belt buckles, and one of Sean's favorites, his old flute. Finn claimed several of these items, especially his father's gold watch and chain and his silver flute.

143

After a long day in the orchard with Hannah and the Indian boys, Finn settled on the porch steps and played Sean's flute. The music was soft and soothing, and in a few moments, his mother came to the doorway and listened with a faraway look in her eyes.

'Been a long time since I heard that flute. Sean stopped playing it after we moved here and began working on the orchards. The last time I remember hearing it was at your wedding.'

Hannah came out carrying Ryan and sat in a chair near Finn listening to the magical music.

'Hear that, Ryan? Your daddy knows how to play a flute just like your grandpa did. Isn't that beautiful?'

The melodies wafted out over the orchards, and soon several of the Indian boys who had been packing fruit for delivery to Chico for the upcoming Fall Festival, were drawn to the porch and sat on the steps below Finn listening in fascination to the music.

When he finished playing, Ipsa asked to see the flute and Finn handed it to him.

'This Fruit Chief's music maker? I remember him play.'

'Yes, that instrument is called a flute. It was one of my father's favorites. He loved to play music with it, and he taught me to play, too.'

Ipsa studied the flute with interest, turning it over and over and fingering the holes that were arranged in two rows.

'Can I blow into flute like you?'

Finn laughed and took the flute.

'Now watch when I put my lips on the end and put my fingers over certain holes. You have to blow into the mouthpiece. Like this.'

And Finn played several bars of music while Ipsa watched with concentration.

'You want to try it, Ipsa?'

He handed the flute to the boy, and Ipsa eagerly put his lips to the end while his fingers tried different combinations. Even his first attempts sounded good, and he handed the flute back with a big grin.

'Can I get flute like that?'

Finn looked at him and smiled.

'Of course, you can, Ipsa. In fact I'll see if they have any in Chico when we go into town for the Festival and if they're not too expensive, I'll get you one.'

Ipsa's eyes widened.

'You would buy for me, Fruit Chief?'

Finn patted him on the back.

'Yes, the next time I go to Chico. I'm glad to see you're interested. Flutes make wonderful music. I'm sure your tribe would appreciate you playing for them once you learn how.

'And by the way, flutes made of bone have been found in caves that are 50,000 years old. Some flutes are side-blown and called piccolos and fifes. End-blown flutes like this one are called Recorders and Tonettes. Flutes are a whole new world of music-making, Ipsa.

'I may have a chance to talk to Jon Simms at the general store at the Fall Festival today in Chico.

* * *

Soon Hannah and Jennifer had their pies and cakes packed in the wagon, and they had on their most fashionable dresses for the Fall Festival.

In town colorful banners were strung across the streets announcing the Fall Festival, and Finn looked in amazement at the number of people on the streets. Finn drove through town and entered the fairgrounds which teamed with men, women, and children, all busy with various points of interest.

Finn stopped at the huge plant display area and deposited several baskets of fresh fruits at his designated spot. He immediately saw that he was one of three fruit-growers on display at the festival. He had a small sign by his produce with 'Kerry Orchards' in large letters.

The women unloaded their cakes and pies with signs on each: apple pie, apple cobbler, apple strudel, apple-plum cobbler, and then their apple, plum, apricot, and pear jams and jellies. They headed for the group of women in a long line of counters full of tasty desserts, and soon had their baked goods and jams and jellies situated in the middle of them with their small 'Kerry Orchard' sign displayed behind cakes and pies. They took turns standing behind the counter waiting for customers and Hannah and Jennifer alternately wandered through the displays looking for something of interest.

Jennifer spied a large display of hand-made quilts, and studied the patterns for some time, certain she could create her own quilt using similar shapes of the patterns she saw. She made notes in her small leather-bound notebook.

When it was Hannah's turn to shop, she walked by many displays, saw children bobbing for apples, and hearing piano music, wandered in that direction.

Three pianos were on display, each played by a professional pianist who seemed to be competing on who could play the loudest, except for the older woman playing the Boisselot Fils piano from France. Her technique was flawless, and Hannah could feel the love that the woman put into her play.

All three pianos were from Europe; A Challen piano from London, and a Gaveau piano of Paris.

Hannah felt proud of her own piano in comparison, even though her's was a hand-me-down from her mother. The piano, a Bosendorfer made in Vienna, Austria had been made in 1830, two years after the company was formed.

Fortunately, because of Finn's reputation, the Kerry name was well-known, the Kerry Orchard's pies and cakes sold quickly to hungry prospectors, and Jennifer and Hannah began to make the rounds together. Soon they found the vegetable competition, and were amazed at the size of the squash, tomatoes, and potatoes on display.

Meantime, Finn watched a match race between two thoroughbred horses from London. Prospectors with plenty of gold dust to spend guaranteed that the betting was fast and furious, and money changed hands faster than Finn could comprehend.

Later in the afternoon, Finn and Hannah danced to lively fiddle music on a small raised platform in the middle of the fairgrounds. Jennifer watched with envy as the two danced, for she and Sean had been avid dancers when they were younger.

Bill Mackey sidled up next to Jennifer as she watched the dancers.

'I'd be right proud to dance a few whirls with you, Mrs. Kerry. What say? Want to give it a try?'

Jennifer smiled, took Bill's hand, and in no time they were dancing right along with the rest of the spirited dancers.

As the evening wound down, they listened to a fiddle contest, amazed at the range and rapidity of the play by several contestants.

Finally, Finn collected the empty baskets of his fruit display, and they loaded their purchases into the wagon and headed home. Tired but satisfied at a fun day at the Festival, they went to bed and slept soundly after their day's activities.

* * *

Finn was as good as his word, and while at the festival in Chico, he found the perfect flute for Ipsa which was not too expensive at a stand set up by Simms' General Store, a good starter flute for a boy.

Later when Finn handed him the flute while the boys worked in the orchard, Ipsa could hardly wait to play it.

'There's one problem with this flute, Ipsa. White men have books of music, and you must learn how to read special notes in order to play their wonderful songs. But you can make up your own music, too, if you prefer. I bought you two books of music just in case.'

Ipsa thought for a minute, and then announced proudly, 'I make up my own music, Fruit Chief–for now. Thank you for gift.'

Soon after Finn heard Ipsa playing his flute while they ate lunch, and eventually other boys wanted flutes, too.

Chapter 24

April-September 1852

In the early spring of 1852, the Maidu Indians experienced a terrible epidemic of cholera, wiping out more than half of the sixty inhabitants of the village. Only a few of the adults survived; among the dead was Chief Sam. Almost all of the younger generation survived since, due to Hannah's urging, they had all been inoculated several years earlier.

A few months after the epidemic, Ruma married Aida, a beautiful Maidu Indian girl of eighteen. When Finn heard the news from his orchard boys, he sought out his friend to give him a gift and his congratulations.

'Pardon me for asking Ruma, but I know nothing of the Maidu marriage customs. How exactly do you go about courting and marrying your new bride-to-be?'

Ruma grunted a laugh and put his hand on Finn's shoulder.

'The white man's way seems easy, for you ask the woman for her hand in marriage, she says 'yes', you have a preacher say the words, and you are married.

'In our culture the path to marriage is more complicated. Aida and me had walked the 'couple's walk' together a number of times, but virgin girls are forbidden to be alone with a man until she is pledged, so one of the women was always nearby. We were never allowed to be alone.

'The suitor–that's me–remains in his family home but sends a gift to the girl's family in the shape of polished shells, usually clam shells which are considered valuable by my people–like gold is in your white man's world. This gift is discussed within the girl's family; if considered insufficient, the gift is returned, but if it is accepted the next phase of courtship begins.

'And, by the way, the girl's consent is usually secured, or at least she is advised of the offer.

'I as the suitor will then visit the father's home and declare my suit over several visits. I simply tell Aida's parents that I would like to have her share my hut. A suitor may bring gifts of food for the family's pleasure. In my case, I brought my normal fish catch and two days' hunting kills to Aida's home with a declaration of intent on my part–although the family was well aware of my intentions by this time.

'When they accepted my gifts I was greatly encouraged, for I felt that Aida also had a hand in the acceptance. After showing my good will toward the family and my capabilities as a hunter and fisherman, I visited their house once more, and played my four-hole flute for them several evenings. Aida joined on occasion with her own flute.

'A separate bed was provided for me near my potential bride. If Aida is willing, we shared a bed, and we are considered *almost* married.

'Ah, but if she refuses to share the bed, she must sit up all night in order to reject me. This was not done with Aida. We were more than ready to share our lives.

'I see,' said Finn, but Ruma put his hand on Finn's chest.

'Wait. I'm not finished yet. We are now sharing a bed, but as a final payment, I must remain with the family for several months, hunting and fishing for them until the father pronounces us *definitely* married. You see in a hunter-gatherer culture like ours, it is important for the suitor to be a good provider. I even captured several wild horses and gave them to Aida's father as a good will gesture.

'And at that point we are ready to build our own home and begin our own family.

'Nothing to it, right, Finn?' he said with a laugh.

'Of course, our tribe is without a Chief now that my father is dead, and her family felt certain that I may be chosen. But this election of a new Chief is a great event, and we must now wait for the selection of our elders.'

In late July, Ruma became the new Chief of the Yamadi Maidu, and at the swearing-in ceremony, he announced that he and Aida would have a new child soon.

By August the plum and apples harvests were underway, and Finn's family was busy with the Maidu boys harvesting the fruit.

The years passed quickly, and Finn realized that the date was August, 1852. The Kerry Orchards had been a lucrative business during the gold rush days, but now many of the prospectors were leaving and the gold that had been pouring from the Sierra Nevada Mountains had drastically fallen off as mining claims were sold at rock bottom prices, mining gear merchants closed their doors, and second-hand mining equipment sold for practically nothing. Mules, once in short supply to prospectors, glutted the market, and mule owners had difficulty selling their stock.

Finn could see by his company ledgers that orders were falling off weekly, and many merchants who were happy to receive Kerry Orchard fruits, were now cancelling contracts or cutting back drastically on orders. Finn's extra wagons and mules were a drag on their profits, and he, like others, looked for ways to economize and sell unused wagons and mules. Luckily for him, the Indian boys still worked diligently in the orchards, and his labor costs were a pittance compared to that of other orchards in northern California–of which there were fewer competitors left as many had disappeared from the scene. The amount of gold the Indian boys brought Finn from time to time had dropped off to nothing lately.

Finn's extra business from the four groups of prospectors along the creeks and streams decreased over night with the dramatic reduction in gold mining, and in his latest check of his business ledger, his $8000 per month had dropped to less than $250 per month, hardly worth the extra effort to deliver the fruits to the prospectors at their campsites.

One evening as Finn remarked on the decrease in business and the seriousness of their reduction in family profits, he listened to his mother's comments with attention.

'Oh, Finn, if only Sean were here, or at least had told us where he hid the gold he got back in 1847. I know he had a lot because I was there when the Indian boys brought us bags of gold nuggets…'

'Mom, we've been over this before. If Dad hid gold around here then surely we would have found it by now. If only he would have confided in you or me before he was killed.'

'Finn,' said Hannah as she held one-year-old Megan and played word games with four-year-old Ryan, 'your Dad was a clever man. If he hid the gold here on the Kerry property, then we will find it. And I can't imagine anywhere else he might have hid it, can you?'

Finn shook his head. 'No, I'm sure you're right, Hannah. Mom, how much gold did you say you thought dad had gathered?'

Jennifer thought for a moment as she took Megan from Hannah and kissed the little blonde girl while she tickled her. Megan screamed, wriggled, and scooted down in Jennifer's lap.

'Well, I remember the boys brought Sean eight bags of nuggets every few weeks, and I remember weighing them on the fruit scales. Each time the boys brought bags, they averaged between two and three pounds of gold. And that went on for two or three months, right up to the time he was shot.'

Finn took a pencil and paper.

'Let's see. Say two-and-one-half pounds per boy for say eight deliveries over three months. That's one-hundred-and-sixty pounds of gold. Wow, that's a lot of gold. And I saw the price of gold on the sign in front of the bank yesterday was $20.67. The price hasn't changed much lately so let's use that number.'

He did more arithmetic and sat back with a smile.

'That's almost fifty-three thousand dollars! Hannah, that would save the orchards with money to spare. We've got to find that gold. Where could Dad hide that much gold on our property?'

'Well, there's the house, and that could take a passel of searching right there,' said Jennifer.

'You're right, mom, But there are other places he could have hid it, too. Like in the tool shed or in the hayloft. Oh, Lordy, you don't suppose the horse ate it, do you?'

They looked at him in surprise, and finally they were all laughing.

'Oh you,' scoffed his mother.

'I'd forget the outhouses. Surely Dad wouldn't be so crude as to hide it there.'

They laughed again.

'Look. Let's do this. You two women concentrate on the house. Look everywhere, and be especially watchful of loose boards or sections of wall that look like they may have been repaired.

'Meanwhile, I'll do a thorough search of the tool shed and hayloft, and even the horse stall. Take your time and do a good job. We'll find that gold yet if we try hard.'

They all felt better after the discussion, and their enthusiasm carried them away.

'Let's start looking tonight, mom,' said Hannah. 'We can take it one room at a time and leave no stone unturned.'

Jennifer nodded her head.

'Okay, I'll take our bedroom, since that seems like a logical place for Sean to hide the gold.'

By eleven o'clock, they had found nothing and were tired and ready for bed.

'Goodnight, Mom. Maybe we'll have better luck tomorrow. We'll find it, I'm sure we will,' said Finn enthusiastically.

* * *

The next day, the Maidu Indian boys did not appear as usual. Finn knew that something might be wrong, but felt he should wait till they returned. One or two days missed did not seem too serious, and he knew that sometimes the boys liked to hunt with their fathers.

Three days went by with no Indian boys. Finn was about to ride to their village when they rode into the yard.

When they arrived to work the orchards, new Chief Ruma approached Finn while the rest waited.

'Four of the Maidu hunters were killed three days ago. Lately they have been forced to travel farther looking for game, and they ran into a group of gold prospectors who thought they were being attacked. Since our hunters have only bows and arrows, the fight was one-sided, and even though the hunters killed two of the prospectors with arrows, all of the hunters died but one who escaped and made his way home.

'Fruit Chief, we need guns! We can no longer fight the white man with bows and arrows. Can you help us get the white man's weapons and teach us to use them?'

Finn thought hard on the subject and finally came to a decision.

'No, Chief, I cannot help you get firearms. Your tactics must be to steer clear of white men while hunting; otherwise, you will cause the white men to band together and fight you. You will lose. There are too many white men and they have the strength of guns. I am sorry, but I do not want to be responsible for the deaths of your people. If you continue in your peaceful ways, your village may survive; otherwise, you will force the white men to organize, and they will destroy your homes and your people.'

Finn knew that the prospectors were now all over the Sierra Nevada Mountains looking for gold, and in the process they were also killing off the game, and what game they didn't get, moved on to other areas where they felt safer, but eventually the game always came into contact with gold-seekers and were soon killed or forced to move on again.

The Maidu hunters were not finding game where they did before, and had to roam in much wider circles which eventually brought them into contact with armed gold-seekers. There was bound to be gun play since the prospectors were afraid of the Indians and felt they were protecting themselves.

The game was only a part of the problem; white men were ruining the streams and creeks with their gold-panning and diversions of water needed by the Indians. The quality of the water suffered, and forced the Indians to find other water sources near their village.

Perhaps, thought Finn, he should suggest a well or two in or near the village.

And because hunting had diminished, the Indians were forced to follow the younger generation and grow their own food. Fields near the Maidu village were now being plowed, and vegetables grew where in the past only grass grew which was consumed by the Indian ponies and the few cattle they kept on hand.

One day the boys came to the porch without Chief Ruma. Finn wondered whether Ruma–Chief Ruma–would still come to the orchards to work with the boys now that he was Chief.

Finn was surprised that the efforts of Hannah had produced such a drastic change in the Maidu culture. Except for history tales told by a few surviving elders, the young men and women would eventually know nothing about the prominence that hunting once had in their culture.

Through Hannah's agricultural efforts, the new Maidu generation had turned almost completely to vegetable growth, and on the side they raised chickens and goats for sources of protein now that the game had practically disappeared. They now got eggs from the chickens, and considered raising cows for milk and cheese, although few of the Indians ate cheese or drank milk.

Finn was also greatly involved in teaching the children how to grow plants, and he was a constant source of information to the Maidu for their expanding agricultural environment. The old ways of the elders to hunt was now a thing of the past, although two or three of the older generation still went on unsuccessful hunts. Hunting was their way of life, and they had difficulty changing their ways.

The younger generation had now developed better methods of making the clay pipe for irrigation than Finn had initially taught them, and he took a few lessons from them to make his clay pipe efficiently and stronger. Finn thought with a grin that the new clay pipe might even survive against the feet of Oakum, the largest Maidu Indian of all, but the most accident-prone.

Finn and his family continued their search for Sean's gold, but in the ensuing weeks found nothing, and their efforts flagged and finally stopped.

In 1853, Finn learned from a newspaper that the Mint in San Francisco (formerly Yerba Buena) now turned gold bullion into official US gold coins. These coins were being sent by California banks to the US National banks in exchange for United States paper currency.

Finn realized that with the changes in the Maidu culture, they must now begin to barter with their products like food and pottery and leather goods. Even the wild horses they continually rounded up in the mountains were a good source of revenue in towns like Chico. Reluctantly, the Maidu made more and more contact with white men, and in the process their culture deteriorated over time. Finn especially noticed this in the clothes the Indians wore, store-bought in Chico and other towns along the Sacramento River.

Finn had already cautioned the Maidu to horde what gold they had because one day economic conditions may force them to use their gold in exchange for the white man's merchandise they may need.

He began to teach them the value of the local paper script that was used in Chico and other towns nearby in place of gold. It was time the Maidu thoroughly understood the value of the gold in their possession in order for them to survive in the white man's world.

Another thing that worried Finn was the fact that California had become a new state in the United States Union. The Maidu may lose everything like Indians in other states had lost their lands and hunting privileges, and may even be forced to leave their homes and move to Indian reservations.

He was sure that that might be the end of the Maidu, unless they continued to develop their skills at farming and growing their own food. Most Indians on reservations refused to accept an agricultural future, and their societies were dying because they would not adapt to the white man's ways of growing their own food.

Chapter 25

October – November 1853

In November of 1853, Jennifer Kerry discussed the deteriorating economy with Finn and in the process she told him how the Maidu Indian boys had brought bags of gold nuggets from a 'magic pool'. The trouble was that Sean never told her where he hid the gold from this pool.

'That was how they described it, Finn, as a magic pool. You should ask them about it. Maybe they will show you the pool and you might find more gold nuggets like Sean did.'

The Maidu boys were surprised when Finn asked them about the pool, for they thought Finn already knew about it from the Fruit Chief. Finn's hopes rose as he saw a chance to find more nuggets in the pool; perhaps he could find enough to prevent selling the orchard property. From the boy's description, the entrance to the pool was almost hidden by a pine tree growing right in front of the rock wall opening. He was curious to see this legendary 'magic pool'.

Finn finally convinced them to take him to the pool, and he followed them up into the low mountains until they had to walk their horses among the scattered rocks. As they rode along next to the high rock wall, one of the boys cried out.

'Someone's here. Look, some of the trees have been cut down.'

They rode into the small pine grove near the high stone wall, and it was obvious that someone had made camp here, for their gear remained in the clearing.

They dismounted, hobbled the horses, and Finn followed the boys along the rock wall face.

They searched among the blankets, saddles, weapons, and food supplies. Finn found a cooking pot on a wooden tripod, and the stew or whatever had been in the pot, was completely boiled away, leaving only a grey scaly crust in the bottom.

'Look, here is a wooden box in the pine grove.'

Finn strode forward and studied the box.

'This is a box of dynamite, boys. Be careful around it. It could explode and kill us all.'

He lifted the lid.

'There are four sticks missing. That could cause an explosion.'

They climbed the hill through the grove to the crevasse entrance, and he looked into the split in the wall.

'The tree over the entrance has been cut down. There is only a stump,' said Ruma pointing at the opening.

Finn saw the stump and glanced up at the entrance between the high rock walls.

'Is this where the pool is, Ruma? With that pine tree covering the entrance, it would be hard to find this place.'

'Yes,' said Ruma. 'We must walk between walls to get to pool. Come.'

Finn followed them into the fissure, and they inched their way along until Ipsa yelled from up ahead in a disappointed voice. They moved forward and stood at the entrance to the pool.

But the pool was gone.

Only a pile of rocks and rubble covered the area where the pool had been. Finn looked around the enclosing rock walls and he could see that an explosion had taken place. Dynamite must have been placed on top of the rock wall near where the boys said a waterfall had existed.

'The pool was right in the center,' said Ruma, 'and the waterfall fell from the top of the wall into the pool. Look, part of the rock face where the water fell, has crumbled, and fallen into the pool, filling it. Only this pile of rubble remains. We could never get to the gold nuggets again. Those huge boulders have filled the pool to the top.'

'And look, Ruma, the waterfall is gone, too; there is no water coming from above,' said Ipsa.

Finn studied the place for a while and asked the boys several questions about how they got the nuggets. Finally, he walked to the wall.

'You say there were steps carved into the stone?'

'Yes,' Ruma said. 'We could climb to the top on the stone steps. But the steps are gone. A large part of the rock face has fallen and broken into pieces to fill the pool. The dynamite must have caused an explosion and brought down a great part of the wall behind the waterfall.'

Finn looked around the rock enclosure.

'Someone was here, probably a gold prospector. They brought dynamite. It was probably them that dynamited the wall, and in the process brought down part of the wall and diverted the stream up above, too. But where are the horses or mules on which they rode here and where are are the men who…?'

'Here,' cried Ipsa who was standing near where the old wall had been.

They rushed to the spot and found an arm sticking out from among the rock rubble. Finn took hold of the hand; it was dry and hard.

'This must have happened sometime ago, boys. I'm surprised that animals didn't find him and make a meal of his arm. And if he's dead, what happened to all his horses and mule? I wonder if some of the men who were here escaped the explosion, saw the results, took the horses and left.'

Ruma looked up and shook his fist.

'The white man has brought ruin to our magic pool, just like he does to everything he touches. Let us leave this place and head home. I must tell my people. They will be greatly displeased.'

'You're right, Ruma. I'd better pack that box of dynamite and take it along or someone or something will set it off and cause another disaster.'

Soon they were on their way down the trail, leaving the magic pool for the last time.

Finn was disappointed, for he had dreams of finding more gold nuggets in the Indian's magic pool.

Hope of finding gold to save his orchards was dashed, and he once more faced a failing economy. Soon he might have to sell the orchards, he thought, but where would he and his family go then? They were in a serious predicament, he realized. His only recourse then might be to turn to law enforcement and accept one of the offers made to him to be a sheriff.

Back at the village, the boys reported what they had seen to the people who shook their heads. One of the surviving elders approached Finn.

'Most white people are crazy. They want to be rich, but their riches are different from ours. His riches are the golden nuggets and gold dust, and they will do anything to get them. The white man won't admit that you only get rich by taking things from other people. They think that if you do not see the people you are stealing from, or you do not know them, or you do not look at them, it is not really stealing.

'Since the beginning of this gold madness, our people have been badly used by the white man; they have stolen our horses, burned our homes, raped our women, ruined our hunting ranges, ruined our water supplies with their gold prospecting, and brought death by diseases to my tribe.

'The Yamadi Maidu have groomed and cultivated oak trees in the forests around us for many years to create a large source of acorns for our winter food. Now the white man cuts down our oak trees to make furniture, they say, and my people will have less winter food. When I met your father, Sean Kerry, I understood his passion for the fruits he grew, and he had even convinced some of us, especially the boys, that starting our own orchards would give us a new source of food, but the trees the boys planted are still young and produce little fruit.'

'Our Yamadi Maidu village in the Sierra Nevada Mountains is a small offshoot from the Nisenan Maidu who lives at the top of the mountains. Our group chose their own chief from among the hunters. Chief Sam, was chosen to lead our people away from the disaster of the Nisenan, where the Konkow Maidu who live on the Sacramento River, plundered and killed. We thought we had escaped their terror, but the white man has taken the place of the Konkow. The Konkow stole from us, raped and kidnapped our women and children, and made life bad for us—until we fled from them and started our own community here. We cannot save our people from these outrages. Perhaps it is time for a new Chief of the Yamadi Maidu to come up with a solution. We do not have the solution to this problem.'

He sat down silently and smoked his pipe while his old wife brought him hot coffee.

'I'm sorry for your losses,' said Finn. 'I wish there were something I could do to make it right, but greedy white men are to blame and they are giving me and my family the same treatment as they give you.'

Finn shook his head, thanked the boys for showing him the pool, and rode for home.

When he got home, Hannah ran out to meet him.

'Finn, two men broke into the tool shed again. I chased them away with the rifle, but they may have taken some of your tools. And your mother was walking in the orchards and noticed another broken fence. Thank God you're home. Where were you? I looked for the Maidu boys, too, but everyone was gone.'

'The boys showed me the magic pool where my father got gold nuggets from the Maidu boys, but white men have destroyed the pool and waterfall, like they do everything.

* * *

In November of 1854, Finn went to the Harvest Moon Festival in Chico. Bill Mackey mentioned to Finn that there was to be a shooting contest at the festival which would last for three days. The top prize was $500 in cash and a rifle or pistol of the winner's choice.

'Sure would like to see you compete, Finn. Would be a great chance for you to make a little extra money,' Bill said.

That was all the prodding Finn needed. He cleaned his pistol and rifle, and was eager to try his skills at the festival.

The shooting contest was to run for three days, so Finn roomed with Bill Mackey so he didn't have to go home each day.

The competition was to be both rifles and pistols, weapons of contestant's choice. One first prize would be awarded for the best combined score of rifle and pistol, and second prize would be either a rifle or pistol. The entry fee was $15.

Bill Mackey convinced him that he'd never have another chance to prove his expertise with his weapons as he would in a contest against other great shooters.

The contest was open to anyone over sixteen, since there were a lot of young men who felt they were experts with their firearms. Because so many men – and even a few women – registered to compete, the contest would be held over three days, the first day being used mainly for zeroing in pistols and rifles only, the second day for pistols, and the third day for rifles.

The Grand prize was $500 plus a rifle and pistol, and second prize was $250 plus a pistol or a rifle, both prizes chosen out of a group of three rifles and three pistols.

The competition was arranged for team play, with up to four shooters per team. This seemed to put Finn at a disadvantage since a team of four could pick the best target out of four, whereas Finn had to go with the targets he shot, meaning that in every round he would be competing against the best of four team members from every team.

This seemed daunting to Finn, but he must abide by the rules.

Drawing from a holster was not part of the competition, but only the resulting array of ten shots in the paper target. Contestants could not rest their weapons on any surface.

There were four shooting positions:
1) pistols at 10 yards
2) pistols at 25 yards
3) rifles at 50 yards
4) rifles at 100 yards

Once the signal was given to fire, the shooter fired 10 rounds in three minutes; this included the time to change cylinders, for many contestants chose the Colt Baby Dragoon as their weapon, or in the case of rifles, this allowed a small time allotment to clean the rifle bore as necessary. If they shot more than 10 rounds, the target was disqualified for that round.

For a team, the best shooter's target was selected by the team leader, placed in an envelope, and that shooter's weapon was put in storage until the next round, so this supposedly kept everyone honest.

The first day was mainly for contestants to zero in their weapons.

The second day was the pistol competition.

Finn carefully cleaned his weapons and loaded the Baby Dragoon and an extra cylinder.

As he waited his turn, Hank, one of the deputies he knew hit him on the shoulder.

'Too bad for you, Finn. This isn't a fast-draw contest. You'd better hit that target good 'cause I'm fixin' to take home that there prize.'

He laughed and Finn smiled.

'Good luck to you, Hank. I mean that.'

Finn was one of the last contestants, and he could see by the results so far that he had his work cut out for him.

He stepped up to the 10-yard line with twenty other shooters.

'Ready on the firing line,' called the referee.

'Fire!'

The noise was deafening, but Finn was prepared, since Bill Mackey told him to put cotton wads in his ears.

Finn fired five rounds just as he did back at the orchards with a good aim and slow squeeze of the trigger. Then he removed the wedge, pulled the barrel off and changed cylinders. He then fired five more shots, taking considerable time with his aim and squeeze. He found that he could easily fire off ten rounds in the allotted time.

'Round complete. Put your weapons on the table, and retrieve your targets.'

Finn did so and looked over his targets carefully. He was satisfied with the results but remembered that he was to be compared to the best of four shooters in each team.

He signed his target, placed his targets in the envelope provided, and handed the envelope to the referee as he came by.

Finn glanced around and realized that there were several shooters like him that were not part of a team of four, but only single contestants.

The 25-yard contest was run exactly like the 10-yard had been.

After firing his ten rounds, he waited until everyone was directed to retrieve their targets.

Again Finn was satisfied with his grouping of hits, and placed the targets in the envelope.

The pistol-shooting went on for about two hours, and the fairgrounds smelled like burnt gunpowder, with thin smoke covering the entire shooting area and the onlooker stands.

After the last pistol group finished, the referee announced that rifle shooting would commence at 2 P.M. tomorrow, starting with the 50-yard targets.

That evening, Bill Mackey watched Finn as he cleaned his pistol and cylinders, and then once again cleaned his rifle. He practiced his reloading technique to be sure he had time to run a cleaning rod through the bore after every two shots. This method allowed him to keep the bore clean for all shots to be fired.

'I admire a man who takes good care of his weapons. Looks like I taught you good, Finn.'

At 2:30 P.M. the next day the 50-yard competition commenced, and each shooter was give five minutes to fire 10 rounds, including any bore-cleaning the shooter felt was necessary. Then weapons were laid down and targets retrieved.

Finn tested the wind as Bill had taught him and made what adjustment he felt necessary for wind and elevation.

After firing, Finn studied his hit patterns and decided he was satisfied, but might make a minor adjustment on the 100-yard competition.

An hour later, the 100-yard competition began, and when Finn studied his targets he was satisfied with his results, so he put the targets in the envelope and handed it to the referee.

After the competition was complete, the judges assessed the selected targets and two hours later announced the results.

'In the pistol competition, the winners are:

In the 10-yard pistol event, Russell Mann and Finn Kerry, a tie, gentlemen.

In the 25-yard pistol event, Finn Kerry

In the 50-yard rifle event Charles Burley

In the 100-yard rifle event, Charles Burley and Finn Kerry, a tie, gentlemen.

'I have to say that ties in a contest like this are rare indeed. And Mr. Kerry has done it twice. Congratulations on a fine competition everyone.'

'The winner of the pistol competition is Finn Kerry.

'The winner of the rifle competition is Charles Burley.

'The judges have decided that the Grand Prize goes to Finn Kerry since he tied for winner in both the rifle and pistol competition and won the pistol contest. Second prize goes to Charles Burley.

'Congratulation to the winners.'

There was a loud round of applause, and several men clapped Finn on the back.

A rugged-looking man with a Marshall's badge on his jacket, walked over to Finn, shook his hand, and grabbed his shoulder.

'That was fine shooting, lad. I'm Marshall Thurston from Stockton. If you're ever interested in a career in law enforcement, look me up. We could use men like you.' He handed Finn a small card with his name and address.

'Thank you, Marshall, but I'm an orchardist by trade. I only learned to shoot to avenge my father's killing.'

Thurston closed his eyelids to slits and studied Finn for a moment.

'Yeah, I heard about you and Polk. You did the right thing there. You could've shot him in the back, but you gave him an even chance. I don't see that sort of thing much anymore. Nice meeting you, Mr. Kerry,' he said, and tipped his hat as he walked away.

In a nearby saloon, Bill Mackey bought Finn a drink.

'Yuh see, Finn? All that there practice paid off. You got two new guns and some drinkin' money, to boot. Congratulations.'

Finn laughed.

'Drinking money? I need to take that $500 back to my wife and family, Bill, and save my orchards. In fact, I may sell both of those guns since I have all I need.'

'Sure, I know'd that. I was jist joshin' yuh.'

Hannah was waiting on the porch for him when he rode in.

'Finn, you were gone three days with no word. I thought maybe you got killed. What happened?'

'I entered a shooting contest that Bill Mackey told me about at the Fall Festival.

'Guess what, Hannah. I won first prize. $500 and a new rifle and new

164

pistol. Bill is going to buy the weapons from me for $75. I was hoping we could hold out a little longer on our mortgage, but we have debts at Simms store that have to be paid, too, and we're going in the hole. Sorry, honey. I didn't realize the contest was for three days. I should have sent word.'

Finn studied his ledger for the third time, and sighed. He knew he had to talk to the family about their deteriorating situation. He didn't look forward to that encounter.

Chapter 26

November 1854

Finn addressed his mother and Hannah after dinner.

'We're not making ends meet since the gold rush tapered off. Prospectors are leaving every day which reduced our fruit deliveries to them to almost nothing; merchants in Chico no longer need the large quantities of fruits they once did, and I am constantly on the lookout for riff-raff breaking our fences, stealing our fruits, and taking my tools.

'Hannah, I have come to a decision. I'm going to take that job in Chico as a part-time deputy for Sheriff Bob Clayton. At least we'll have a little more income, and it will only be for a little while till we can get on our feet again.'

'Oh Finn, you're not cut out to be a lawman. You're an orchardist, you love growing things and so do I. Why put yourself and us at risk by taking a low-paying job where some drunken prospector might shoot you down at any time?'

Finn hugged her and kissed her, ran his fingers up and down her back.

'I don't think it's as bad as all that, Hannah, but I have to do something. With a little income we just might make it.'

She put her hand on his shoulder and smiled.

'Well, I have some good news for a change. I've been thinking about a dog for Ryan, and...'

'Honey, we can't afford a dog right now. That will have to wait. I'm sure Ryan will understand. And besides, he's only six years old. Let's wait till he's a little older.'

Hannah ignored his comment, turned, left the room, and returned holding a box. She looked at Finn with those mischievous eyes of hers and a pleading look on her face, and he melted. He opened the lid, glanced inside, and saw the fluff-ball of a Labrador puppy.'

'Hannah,' he groaned.

'Jon Simms *gave* him to me, Finn. He's the runt of the litter. He'll probably never get very big, and…'

'You mean you got him for nothing? That's not like Jon Simms. Does he have worms or something?'

She laughed.

'Of course not. You can see just by looking at him that he's healthy. He was the last one, and Jon got tired of listening to him whine, and felt like he needed a home…so he gave him to me.'

'Well, the price is right. I just hope he doesn't eat much. A small dog is a good move, Hannah. Ryan will love him.' He kissed her.

She walked off with the box, smiling from ear to ear.

The last thing Finn heard was:

'Ryan, Ryan, look what Daddy bought for you.'

How can a man get mad at a woman like that? He wondered with a smile.

Although Ryan and the Lab became inseparable, the dog still had an attraction to Finn. Finn was immediately embarrassed by the dog, since he followed Finn everywhere if Ryan worked in the orchard planting trees or did early morning chores. Whenever anyone wanted the dog, they simply looked for Finn. No one had yet come up with a name for the Lab, but in a short while his size presented them with the perfect name for the yellow dog 'runt-of-the-litter' …

'Big'.

* * *

Finn rode into Chico the next morning and talked to the new sheriff, Bob Clayton, about the deputy job.

'You understand it would only be three days a week, don't you Finn? I wish I could hire you full time, but I just don't have that kind of budget, and besides the rowdies seem to be disappearing from the area with the gold rush simmering down. You've got a good reputation with your gun, so I'm authorized to give you some work; some of the merchants suggested it, especially Jon Simms, but I may have to let one of my regular deputies go soon if my budget don't pick up.'

And so Finn Kerry became a deputy on Friday through Sunday since most of the trouble-makers came to town on weekends.

Three weeks later, Finn was on the job early on a Friday morning. He was told to walk the business section every two hours as he put in his ten-hour day. The regular deputy and the sheriff took the late-night duty. Occasionally Finn would have to jail a drunk or break up bars fight, or knock a head with his pistol barrel, but that was about the size of his job. He was glad that the prospectors were leaving and the town was getting quiet again, even though it might mean he would lose his job.

He told Bob Clayton that he had to stop in at the bank on his lunch hour to discuss his mortgage. He didn't think it would take long, but he wanted the sheriff to know where he was, just in case.

As he entered the small bank, he glanced around at the number of people lined up at the window. A few men seemed disinclined to wait in line, probably waiting for the line to go down, he thought, so they simply stood at the center table where the bank's forms were located. Two of the men Finn didn't recognize, but supposed they were prospectors exchanging gold for bank notes for making payments here in Chico, so they didn't have to carry gold dust everywhere in town.

The bank manager, Mr. Stillman, beckoned him into his office. Finn sat facing him while Stillman pulled out Finn's file and studied the sheets carefully.

'Looks like you've been making your payments right on time, Finn. I understand how your business is hurting with the economic downturn, but I guess that's affecting everyone. Sheriff Clayton told me about the deputy job. I only wish he could hire you full-time.' He laughed. 'A banker always feels safer with a good gun to rely on, you understand...'

Stillman showed Finn the ledger and showed him his balance. Finn knew they still had several years left before the mortgage would be paid off in full.

There was a commotion outside the office in the bank, and Stillman peeked out his special peep-hole. He turned around to Finn.

'Finn, there's a robbery in progress! They may try to get me to open the safe. Are you…yes, you're armed. What do you think we ought to do? They'll be in here in a minute. Please, I don't want any gun play in my bank; people could get hurt or killed.' Stillman looked on the verge of panic.

Finn put out the light in the office and pulled down the window shade. He climbed on the file cabinet by the window between the office and the main bank area and peeked over the smoked-glass upper edge.

The two men he'd seen standing by the table had guns out and had everyone in the bank lying on the floor with their hands behind their backs. One of the men was taking money and coins from the female bank teller while the other one headed for the manager's office.

Finn hopped down and hid behind the door. 'Here he comes, Mr. Stillman,' Finn said as he drew his pistol.

The door jolted open, and the gunman came in with gun drawn.

'You the bank manager? 'Cause I'd like you to open your safe…'

Finn stepped out from behind the door, pushed it shut, and hit the man on the head with his pistol.

The man turned, but fell to the floor unconscious.

'You have something to tie him up with, Mr. Stillman? I'm going to see if I can hogtie that other fella out there before someone gets hurt. Just keep quiet and let me handle this, okay?'

Stillman was in shock, and nodded mechanically as he watched Finn go to the door. Obviously, Stillman had never had a gun pointed at him before, and he was petrified.

Out in the bank, the lone gunman had finished gathering money from the teller and held his gun on the rest of the customers. Impatient, he turned toward the manager's office and yelled.

'Eli, what's going on in there? You got that safe open yet?'

He edged toward the manager's door while watching the people on the floor, and started to open it when Finn threw the door open, put his gun barrel against the man's forehead, and closed the door quietly.

'Drop your gun!'

The man's eyes grew large and he looked Finn in the eyes, started to raise his gun, thought better of it, and dropped the gun to the floor.

'You two working alone? I mean, is there anyone else out there who is part of your gang?'

'No…no sir. It's just the two of us.'

'Fine. Now I'd like you to join your friend, Eli, there on the floor. Do it quiet please and you won't get hurt.'

Finn kept his pistol barrel against the man's head as he slowly sank to the floor while staring at the barrel of Finn's gun in his face, and flattened out like his partner.

'Hands behind your back,' Finn said with authority.

The man complied and Finn used his handcuffs. Finn glanced at Stillman.

'I reckon you'd better send your teller for Sheriff Clayton, Mr. Stillman. I'll stay here with these two till he sends some deputies over.'

Finn could see that Stillman was sweating and wiping his head with his handkerchief. The poor man was in a state of shock. His hands were shaking badly.

'Why don't you set in your chair a spell, Mr. Stillman, and I'll pour you a glass of that water over there. Fact is, I could use a glass myself, if you don't mind. What's your teller's name? I'll send her for Sheriff Clayton.

'Her name's Rita,' said Stillman stuttering like a mechanical man.

'You just keep an eye on these two fellas for a minute.'

Finn went out and told the people on the floor to get up.

'We have everything in hand now. You can go about your business.'

Finn talked to Rita who was flustered after the episode with the gunman at her window. She began to cry and Finn held her shoulder to calm her. She nodded at his words, and Finn returned to the office, sat in the chair he had occupied before the bank holdup, and stretched his legs out in front of him. He looked down at the two tied men as Stillman handed him water.

'Well now, your partner's name is Eli. And what's your name? And fill in the last name, if you please.'

The man glanced over at Eli who was still unconscious and shrugged his shoulders.

'He's Elijah Polk and I'm…'

Finn jumped out of the chair and brought his pistol out.

'Polk? Well, ain't that something? Okay, what's your name?'

'Caleb. Caleb Polk.' He turned his head and looked up at Finn. 'What? Why are you acting so surprised?'

Finn shook his head and looked at Stillman without seeing him. 'By damned. The Polk brothers. Just like Bill Mackey said would happen someday. He said to watch my back because Jed Polk might have some kin about somewhere,' he said with a laugh, 'and here you are.'

'You mean…Are you the Kerry what shot my brother?'

'Yep. That's me, Caleb. And I gave your brother an even chance to shoot me, too, but I was a might luckier.'

'Well, I'll be. We don't mean you no harm, Mr. Kerry. Didn't even know you wuz in Chico. Jed was a pain in the butt if you ask my family. Jed was what you call the black sheep of the family.'

Finn laughed.

'Caleb, you don't seem to be a whole lot better. But at least you're alive. Remember that. I could have killed both of you, and been a hero to boot.'

A commotion in the outer bank made Finn glance toward the manager's door and swing his pistol that way, too. It opened slowly and Sheriff Clayton peeked in, and then he and two deputies entered with shot guns and pistols drawn.

'Come in Sheriff. Here's two Polk brothers ready for a peaceable walk over to your jail. Right, Caleb?'

'Did you say Polk? The sheriff asked.

'Yep, guess we got two more Polks off the street.'

The lawmen sized up the situation and the deputies marched the two desperados across the street to the jail, supporting the groggy Eli Polk between them, while Bob Clayton asked questions of Stillman and Finn.

'I have to hand it to you, Finn, stopping a bank robbery without firing a shot. That's one for the books, all right. We'd better check our WANTED posters and see if there's any rewards for these two bank robbers. Could possibly be some money in it for you.'

In a week the news was all over the territory about Finn Kerry stopping a bank holdup without firing a shot. Finn got a few free drinks out of it and thought that was the end of it, but Sheriff Clayton talked to him one evening as he was about to go off-duty.

'Talked to some of the Chico merchants about you, Finn. And just so you know, one of my deputies, Paul Walker, is movin' to Yerba Buena as a deputy there. His wife has folks living near there and she wanted to be closer to the family.

'Banker Stillman was emphatic about hiring you. Said he's never seen a lawman with more guts and common sense than you showed in that holdup. So if you're a mind to, that full-time deputy job is open to you. What d'ya say, Finn? Interested?'

'Sure am, at least till we get our orchards back in shape. Mr. Stillman is reducing my mortgage payments a bit as a sort of reward to help us balance our budget, and I don't mind riding back and forth from our place to Chico. In fact, that's a nice ride. Um, how much does the job pay, Bob?'

Bob Clayton laughed and told him, and Finn squirmed a bit.

'Bob? Pat Ehrens told me that some of the Chico citizens want me to run for sheriff. I'm embarrassed to tell you, but you never mind. I thought on it and said no.

'That would mean I'd have to move into town and give up my orchards, Bob. I couldn't do that. Those orchards are our future, Hannah and me and the kids. My boy, Ryan, is already planting small trees at seven years of age, and I can see that someday he'll make a fine orchardist. And besides, I doubt that I could beat you in an election, Bob.

'I thanked Pat Ehrens for telling me about their confidence. I never realized what I was getting into when I let Bill Mackey teach me to shoot. I've been getting offers from several towns along the Sacramento River lately. I guess killing a pest like Polk gives a man a certain reputation. And now we have two more Polks in jail, and nobody got hurt.

'However, I've sold my book, and Hanford Publishing wants me to travel to several cities around the country and do some book promotion. I may have to take off any time now. Can you handle that? Probably wouldn't be gone more than a few days at a time. What d'ya think, Bob?'

'Not a problem, Finn. Do what you have to, but let me know in advance so's I can adjust the schedule with the other deputies. And good luck with yer book.'

Finn walked away while the Sheriff stood there and watched him go, shook his head, tipped his hat back, walked off toward the sheriff's office, and laughed all the way.

'Book publishing. Now I've got a deputy who writes books.'

Chapter 27

July 1855

The Kerry Orchards were almost broke by July, 1855. Finn was gone most of the time with his deputy job, and Ipsa and Hannah directed operations in the orchards. At the moment they were almost through with the first apricot harvest of the year, and Hannah was certain they had more fruit than they could sell in Chico or anywhere. The orchards were producing well, but there were simply no buyers for fresh fruit.

With the help of the Maidu Indians, Jennifer and Hannah learned to set snares and traps for small animals to provide meat for the family. Even seven-year-old Ryan Kerry could set a good snare. This was an expedient because Finn was living in town and did not have time to hunt, and the Maidu boys were now busy with their own growing with apple trees, a few apricot trees, corn and other vegetables.

Gold prospectors had ruined the game hunting all through the Sierra Nevada Mountains, so hunting was fruitless. Jennifer, Hannah, and Ryan went through the motions of setting traps, but seldom caught anything. When Finn had a spare minute to hunt, he tried to bring down a deer, but it ran just as he fired, got away, and Finn didn't have the time to chase it. Hannah and his mother were all ready to skin it, and were disappointed when Finn didn't bring the deer home.

After Finn took the job as deputy, Hannah studied the business ledger and realized how desperately low on cash they were. She finally made a resolution.

All day, for two days, Hannah played her Bosendorfer piano, going through many of her music scores while Jennifer was busy in the kitchen, listening to the wonderful music, but curious about what had gotten into Hannah. On the third day, Hannah presented herself to Jennifer with resolve.

'Mom, I've decided. I'm going to sell my piano.'

'Hannah. No. But why?'

'Because we're almost broke, mom.' She nodded her head. 'Yes. I'm certain. For the last two days I've played about every song I ever knew, and now I'm ready to sell it. It's been in my family for as long as I can remember. My mother used to play it and taught me to play. It was one of the only things that I brought to our wedding.' Tears rolled down her cheeks, and she bowed her head.

Jennifer could see what a great sacrifice this was for the girl. She patted her on the back, and then hugged her.

'You'll get a new one someday, Hannah. You wait and see. These bad times will soon be over. I think that's a wonderful sacrifice you're making to save the orchards.'

When Hannah talked to Jon Simms at the general store about selling her piano, he immediately thought of someone who was looking for a good piano, a woman named Cecelia Trask, one of the leading women in the social circle of Chico. Her husband was a successful farmer with land adjacent to the Kerry orchard property. So with resignation Hannah parted with her favorite instrument.

Simms came with two men in a large wagon to take the piano, and Hannah couldn't watch them as they loaded the beautiful old instrument. As they drove away, she ran to the porch and watched them until they were out of sight, and then she sat on the front porch and cried while the children and Jennifer tried to console her.

When Finn came home from being part-time deputy, he immediately noticed the empty space in the parlor where the piano had been. He went to Hannah and hugged her in a long embrace.

'Hannah, mom said you sold your piano. Honey, I know what a sacrifice that was for you to lose your piano. But one day soon I'll make it up to you and get you a brand new piano, the best that money can buy. I'm so sorry, honey. I'll miss your piano, too.

'But there's a bright side to this, Hannah. The money you got for your piano will make three payments on our mortgage. That'll stretch us out till about September.

'It's these blasted property taxes. Since the gold rush began, Butte County has been expanding their services and had the population to support the additions. Now all the prospectors are disappearing, and the county budget can't keep up with the increases. Their budget won't balance any more than ours will, so they upped the property taxes and we don't have any way to meet them.

'Look, honey, we're going under; it's as simple as that. Three more payments will keep us afloat for a few more months and then what? The only way I could make any more money would be to become Chico Sheriff. And I wouldn't feel right about running against Bob Clayton. He's bent over backward to give me work as a deputy. I just couldn't do that to him. And besides, we'd have to live in town, too, and probably have to sell the orchards anyway. That's not a good solution for us. If he were out of the picture, I may consider running, but that's the only way.

'Miles Bracken's kids see a chance to take the orchards away from us and sell them again if we can't make the payments on the mortgage. If we had Daddy's gold, I could buy our orchards outright, but I don't know where he hid it. That means we have to sell the orchards before a foreclosure takes place or we'll lose everything.

'I just want you to be aware of what I'm thinking. I talked to Banker Stillman the other day at lunch about the possibility of selling the orchards before his bank forecloses. He thought if I was really serious, he would talk to Brett Trask, the farmer who owns the large acreage next to us. He's made inquiries with the bank about our orchards. I guess he suspects we're going under. For some reason, he wants our land, maybe to expand his farm. But Stillman says Trask may want us to clear the unused acreage of stumps before he'd be interested in buying. Dang it! That would just put *another* burden on us. There's lots of huge stumps out there on that unused fifteen acres, most of them big old oak trees. I don't know how I would ever get that field cleared before the foreclosure.'

'Did you say Trask? I think that's the one who bought my piano. Cecelia Trask.'

* * *

A week later Finn was almost home from a long day in Chico when he heard a shot, and spurred his horse into the orchards where the shot came from. He found Hannah standing proudly over a dead deer with their dog, Big, standing with a foot on the deer's head. Her latest pregnancy was showing now. Finn looked down at Big who was seventy-five pounds, hardly the runt Hannah had obtained from Simms for free. Big bounded over to Finn.

'Honey, you shouldn't be out here hunting in your condition. The Indians will catch deer for us. They're out here hunting a couple of times a week.'

He realized how the family struggled to survive during the severe economic conditions. Finn's salary was not taking care of the mortgage, even after Banker Stillman reduced the payments after the bank robbery attempt as a reward for Finn saving his bank.

He hopped off his horse and embraced Hannah while Ryan and Megan looked on. He picked Megan off the ground and twirled her around till the little girl screamed with ecstasy.

'Looks like we have *two* hunters in the family, honey...oops, make that three hunters, right Ryan? You've been doing well with your animal snares, too. Your mother told me about your exploits out beyond the orchards.' He glanced over at his wife. 'Hannah honey, you did good.'

Finn draped the dead deer over his saddle and they walked up to the house with Big running alongside nipping at the deer's head. Later Jennifer and Hannah skinned the deer, prepared the meat for short-term storage, and pegged out the deer skin for scraping, knowing they could barter the hide with Jon Simms for food supplies.

They retired to the porch, and Finn sat on the steps in the late afternoon, played the flute, and Hannah sat on the porch with his mother, Ryan, and Big, and listened. Megan scooted into Finn's lap and snuggled into his arm, making it a challenge for him to play. He stopped playing at an interlude, hugged Megan and set her on his lap facing outward. The Indian boys came from the orchards to listen, too. Jennifer put her hand on Finn's shoulder.

'Finn you play as well as Sean did. Having that flute is almost as good as having Hannah's piano.'

177

'This flute could never take the place of Hannah's piano.' Finn looked at his wife. 'Some day we'll get you a new one, honey, when our ship comes in. I promise.'

'By the way, have you thought of a name for our new baby?' Finn asked.

'Yes, if it's a boy, I'd like to name him after my Daddy, Patrick Dennis Kerry. If it's a girl, I'd like to name her Katherine Ann, after my grandmother, and we'll call her Katie.'

Finn looked at her and smiled.

'Katie. I like that. Katie Kerry,' he mused. 'I like the sound of that.'

Finn stopped playing as he saw a horse approaching at a fast trot. Finn recognized Deputy Ralph Forbes from Chico. Finn rose from the porch and stepped down into the yard.

'Ralph? What brings you out our way? Aren't you on duty this evening?'

'Finn, there's been a killing in town. Some drunk gunman done killed Sheriff Bob Clayton. Some of the citizens thought you'd better be notified. I'm sorry to be the one who brung you this news, Finn.' He turned his horse and rode off waving. 'Have to get back to town, Finn. Things are in an uproar there. Some folks want to lynch the drunk who shot Bob.'

Finn looked off into the distance and realized what this might mean to his family. Now Finn would have to run for sheriff or be nominated quickly by the Chico city council. Whichever way it went, Finn would now be Sheriff Kerry of Chico.

In the hectic days that followed, the Chico city council elected Finn to be the *interim* sheriff until a new sheriff could be elected. Finn knew the council would now drag their feet since they would figure they had the job of Sheriff covered. But at least he would be receiving the full sheriff's salary. Finn would have to live in town until a new sheriff was elected, which might be months away. That meant he would only see his family about once or twice a month – unless he moved them all into town. And he knew that wouldn't work since the orchards needed tending. He was caught from both ends.

* * *

178

The Maidu culture was changing drastically due to the disappearance of game throughout the Sierra Nevada Mountains. Because of the threat of gun fights with white men roaming the mountains looking for gold, the Maidu were no longer safe when hunting; from bad experiences, they knew that bows and arrows were no match for the rapid-fire action of the white man's weapons, and they did not have the funds to buy those weapons even if they could find a source to sell them to the Maidu. They were caught in an awkward position.

When Hannah began teaching the Maidu boys and girls to plant and grow corn and other vegetables, she had not foreseen the near future when hunting was no more a major part of their culture.

Now their livelihood centered on what they could grow, and Finn and Hannah began to teach them how to increase their food yields while keeping their fields fertile and full of nutrients.

The first part of their education dealt with rotation of crops so that fields used for a vegetable this year lay fallow the next season. In this way the fallow fields rejuvenated the soil with nutrients and prepared it for the next planting.

Finn explained reasons for rotation: Plant diseases are controlled and reduce the spread of these diseases; insects are controlled, and insect infestations are reduced; and nutrient balance is enhanced: different plants provide different nutrients and keep soil from being depleted; some plants enhance the soil, so rotation produces free organic soil conditioning.

The Maidu caught on to this quickly, and soon the fields around their village were using plant rotation exclusively.

The second part of increasing their yields turned out to be a benefit to both the Maidu and to Finn Kerry. This involved the use of fertilizer on their plants, and here was where the Maidu were fortunate.

The Yamadi Maidu always had many horses, mostly wild ponies, and Finn saw immediately as the Maidu became more reliant on their crops for subsistence, that their horses were a great source of fertilizer. The question was how to use this source.

Finn was aware of the composting idea since his family had used this method of creating fertilizer for years, but as orchardists, they had few horses and other livestock from which they could increase their fertilizer yields.

He studied the literature on composting and soon found the perfect answer for the Maidu and for him, also. He showed the Maidu how to build multiple bins in a row to store the manures from their horses and the many chickens, cows, and goats they had gathered.

Interestingly, composting of the manure reduced the total volume of the pile by about fifty percent, which made the fertilizer much easier to handle and nutrient-rich.

The location of these bins was important, and the best place to build them was close to their horse corrals so that fresh manure could be transferred to the bins on a continuing basis. Even their chicken houses and fenced yards could be located near the compost bins.

The location had to be on high ground so that water could run off and not cause a slimy mess. Low sloped hillsides turned out to be best, for the horses could have fresh food on the grasses, and water would run off away from the bins, leaving them with just the right amount of moisture.

Even the chickens benefited because Finn learned that by moving their feeding yard every month brought them in contact with fresh food in the ground. Moving their housing and fences was not easy, but they soon learned to make their fencing more mobile.

The tools needed for composting consisted of a wheelbarrow, a manure pitch fork, a shovel, and as Ipsa suggested, a clothespin for the nose. These were standard tools sold by Jon Simms at the general store, and Finn was able to acquire four sets of these tools for the Maidu as they developed their composting system.

The bins were constructed of medium-sized, straight timbers with slight air spaces between courses. Each bin had one wall between each successive bin. The multiple bins allowed for *new* compost, *decomposing* compost, and *finished* compost which could be used after about a month right on plants.

Each bin had a center clay pipe standing vertically with numerous air holes about one-inch in diameter to allow the compost to 'breath' or aerate. The Maidu became experienced clay pipe makers using a process similar to that used by Finn for his irrigation pipe, but in a much larger diameter.

The various bins used a simple skin cover, employed a *turning phase* which was a tough job, not to mention, smelly, and a *watering phase* whereby each week or as weather demanded, the compost piles were watered to keep the moisture level up.

New manure was watered before being added to the first bin. The fertilizer created with this system was usually ready within a month or two with good management methods. The young Maidu tribe quickly developed a well-organized fertilizer system, even adding the leaves from the many trees surrounding their village. The young men and even some of the women took turns at turning the compost in the second stage, a smelly job but necessary for good compost.

When done properly the composting bins had an 'earthy' smell that was not unpleasant.

The benefits of the composting system were far-reaching, for not only the manures of horses and chickens were used, but table scraps could be added with care so as not to draw rats or other pests. This created new waste disposal methods for the Maidu who in the past had been unsanitary with their food waste.

The resulting fertilizer was good for all of the Maidu crops, and they developed such a large amount of fertilizer that several wagon-loads of this fertilizer were delivered to Finn at the orchards every month. So Finn's efforts to help the Maidu increase their crop yields was a no-cost fertilizer gift from the Maidu to Finn.

Finn's next step involved the Maidu Indian's gold. California had become the 31st state on September 9, 1850, and he was sure that soon the Indian lands would be confiscated, and the Indians would be put on reservations as had happened in other states. He had already heard talk in that direction. Whether the Maidu would need financial help or not depended on how generous the U.S. government would be.

He wasn't certain how much gold they had scattered among the tribal members, but he talked to Chief Ruma and explained that eventually they might need to use this gold for their own survival if the government did not deal fairly with them.

Finn suggested Chief Ruma gather all of the gold in the tribe and let Finn put it in the bank in Chico, and give Finn power of attorney in case they might need this financial aid in the future. Ruma understood the way Indian treaties had been disregarded in the past, and agreed with Finn.

Within a week Finn deposited $45,355 in gold in Stillman's bank.

Chapter 28

July 1855

Farmer Brett Trask stood on his front porch; listened to his wife play her new piano, looked out over his ripened corn crop, and sighed with contentment. He was a big man with a bald head, muscular arms, and a wide nose. Soon he would add the Kerry property to his holdings, but he had no immediate plans to do anything with the acreage. At the moment he was waiting for Finn Kerry to put the property up for sale. According to Banker Stillman this may happen soon. He was certain that the Kerry Orchards were going broke, and he wanted to help this trend along as much as possible so Finn Kerry would sell him their land. Trask wanted to make it as tough on Finn as possible. The steep property tax was one way to whittle Finn down. Keeping Finn in the Sheriff's job was another way. He had talked to his friends on the Chico city council and tried to convince them that they had the best man as sheriff, so why would they need to elect a new one? Trask knew that Finn missed his family, and could not spend the time he needed in the orchards keeping the fruits healthy. Kerry Orchards had continually lost customers during the trying days after the gold rush had petered out.

Trask thought he might keep the orchards producing as long as everything was in good shape, but he had no long-term plan formulated yet. He knew that Ruma, the new Maidu Chief and his young bride would continue to tend the orchards if he could pay them. Their wants were simple: food, clothing, vegetable seeds, perhaps a new plow and maybe a mule. He could easily afford that.

His main concern was finding Sean Kerry's gold without arousing suspicions.

He smiled when he thought how easily the information had come to him. One of the Maidu Indian boys worked for Brett Trask, helping him bail hay on his farm which was next to the Kerry Orchards. In talking to the Indian boy while they took a lunch break, Trask learned through a slip of the boy's tongue of the gold nuggets the boys had been giving Sean Kerry before he was killed. The Maidu Indians were so closed-mouthed that acquiring the information was like a gift from the blue.

Trask realized that somewhere on the Kerry property, a sizable quantity of gold was hidden, and if Finn Kerry and his mother and wife knew where it was, they would be using it to improve their lives and pay off the mortgage. Therefore, they *didn't* know where it was.

Trask knew that somehow he must get that property. He began to plan in that direction. He was furious with his wife for buying Hannah Kerry's piano, since it gave the Kerry family a three-month reprieve before they were hard pressed for funds to pay any of their bills, especially their mortgage.

He knew that the increased property taxes were weighing heavily on the Kerry family.

And Finn's orchards were not producing as much as they were. Finn had been selling spare equipment in order to reduce his overhead expenses. The Indian boys under Chief Ruma were still tending the Kerry orchards, but without Finn's guidance, the trees were not as productive as they once were. And Finn's customer base had shrunk to almost nothing.

Trask smiled. It was just a matter of time before he had the Kerry property. And time was on his side.

* * *

Late one evening, Finn called a family meeting in the parlor on one of his few nights home.

'I've been over our finances six ways from Sunday looking for some way to pay these outrageous new property taxes, but I can't see any way around it. We'll have to sell Kerry Orchards. I'm sorry. I wish I had better news.'

Groans of despair met his announcement, and Jennifer hugged him as did Hannah.

'Isn't there anything else we can do, Finn?' asked Hannah.

'Afraid not, Hannah. We're broke and living on credit at Simms' store as it is. My sheriff's salary is just keeping our heads above water, and I've already inquired of the Chico city council about a raise, but they resisted, saying that the city budget was already in trouble.'

Once Finn announced to Banker Stillman that the Kerry orchards were going up for sale, Stillman relayed the information to Brett Trask. Trask now jumped at the chance to make an offer to Finn. The offer was extremely low, and Trask demanded that Finn remove all the stumps on the unused acreage as part of the contract, knowing this would put Finn in an even worse bind to accomplish. He was sure that Finn would have a hard time finding another buyer in these economically bad times. Trask was in a superior position.

Finn was notified by the banker of Trask's offer and conditions.

Finn disliked Brett Trask; a man who didn't take good care of his animals was untrustworthy in Finn's mind. While on his lunch hour, Finn visited Stillman at the bank, and asks him his opinion of Trask.

'Well, the man pays his bills on time, and that farm of his is making money. He has no mortgage on the place, and as I remember, he was asking about any new properties near his that he might acquire to expand his farm. I mentioned your orchards going up for sale and he sounded interested, almost like he'd been waiting for you to sell. Seems like a marriage made in heaven, Finn.'

Finn's mood was dismal; he was now away from home when the orchard work took place, and could only get home once or twice during the month.

Chapter 29

July 1855

Finn talked to the Maidu Indians and asked for help in removing all the stumps in the last unused fifteen acres. Finn asked Ruma to supervise the work, since he would be in Chico as interim sheriff until a new sheriff was elected.

'Brett Trask is driving a hard bargain for our property. But I have no alternative now since I have no other buyers, and I have to sell before the bank forecloses. This is that 'rock and a hard place' I told you about.

'I need eight or ten men to clear the stumps out of my fifteen acres, Chief. Can you spare them?'

Chief Ruma nodded. Ruma agreed to help him and selected ten boys to do the work, including Oakum who is a giant of a man now eighteen years of age.

'You have been a great friend to me and my people, Fruit Chief. Anything we can do to help you and your family, we do. When do we start?'

Finn shook his hand.

'As soon as you can, Chief. My mortgage is due at the end of next month, so I only have about six weeks to clear the fields. Think you can manage that? There's some mighty big stumps out there.'

'Yes, we will have done by end of this month. I will bring Oakum; he is strongest man in tribe. We will bring strong horse, too. I remember big stumps in those fields. My father told me of the huge oak trees that once stood on that land. Those were once part of the trees we groomed for our acorns, our winter food supply. Some were over one-hundred years old. Too bad they had to be cut down, but that is the white man's way. He does not enjoy beautiful trees, but only the jingle of coins in pocket.'

They laughed and Finn rode home satisfied that the fields would be cleared on time.

* * *

Five days later, Finn rode home early from Chico and passed his mother, Hannah and the children as they headed for town to do the weekly shopping.

'How're the boys doing with the stumps, Hannah? Are they making progress?'

She looked up at him sitting on his horse, her handsome, gentle man, she thought.

'I think so, Finn. They have a huge bonfire going in the middle of the field and there's a bunch of stumps burning. We're off to do our shopping. We'll be back by dark.'

They waved, and Finn rode on toward home.

When he arrived, he rode to the fields where the stumps burned in a towering inferno, smoke covering the whole area like a low heavy fog. He sized up what they had done and looked again in surprise. Only three bulky stumps remained, but they were giant-sized, and he knew that they would have a job getting them out. He waved to Chief Ruma and the Indian boys, and rode on to the house.

He washed up and from the kitchen he could hear the axes chopping at the stumps. Once in a while he heard one of the boys yell. He pulled out his financial ledger, studied the front cover, and then put it down again, knowing that balancing his books for the Kerry Orchards was over; the property would be sold in a few more days to Brett Trask, now that the stumps would be cleared.

He heard more yelling from the field and strolled out on the porch. He watched the huge bonfire blazing, smoke rising to cover the valley below like a curtain. From his position, it looked like all the stumps were out except one, and all the boys had gathered around Oakum as he put his back against the stump while the horse pulled at the other side.

187

Oakum was yelling something. Now they were all pushing at the stump as they struggled to free it from the earth. The stump was about six feet long and six feet in diameter. He watched with interest as they rolled the huge stump out of the hole onto its side, and a great cheer went up. They were obviously happy that the last stump was finally out, thought Finn.

He squinted against the setting sun. Finn crossed the porch and walked down the steps toward the field where Oakum and the other boys had gathered around the huge stump. The boys were yelling and waving at Finn and in a moment he was running across the field to the stump.

Oakum yelled to Finn and waved his arms. Finn hurried over to this last monstrous stump. A small head poked out of the hollow center. It was Selum, one of the smallest boys working in the field. He saw Finn, beckoned him closer, and pointed down into the heart of the old tree. Finn stooped over the great oak stump and peered into the darkness within, but he could see nothing. It was too dark. Selum pulled his knife from its scabbard, scrambled back into the immense cavity, and Finn could hear him scraping, chopping, and rooting about deep inside. Selum's head popped out of the hole surprising Finn. The boys were all standing around the huge stump. Selum laughed as he held out something in both hands.

It was a small bag, Finn thought. Selum grunted and handed the bag to Finn, and when Finn grabbed it in one hand, he almost dropped it because of the weight.

Finn looked at the leather bag for a moment; a bag which Finn guessed was about five inches by three inches by three inches. He turned it over and saw the leather thong tied at the top. He undid the thong. The bag was heavy, maybe twenty-five or thirty pounds, thought Finn, a lot of weight for such a small bag. He put it on the ground and several yellow stones rolled out of the opening. Finn looked again.

They were gold nuggets!

The boys had found Sean Kerry's gold. For a moment he was elated, and then he realized that there was only one bag, and he hid his disappointment.

Chief Ruma walked over and stood beside Finn and put his hand on Finn's shoulder.

'Is that it, Fruit Chief? Is that your father's gold?'

Finn glanced at the Chief and nodded.

'I am surprised,' said Finn. 'I thought there would be more…From the weight I would guess this is about thirty pounds. That's…about $10,000. Not bad, but not enough to pay off my mortgage. From the description my mother gave me, I thought the boys had given my father more.' He looked at the nuggets and shrugged.

'Yes,' said Ruma. 'I remember the Maidu giving your father sixteen pounds of gold that first day, and about twenty-four pounds more a few days later. Over several months the Maidu gave him more, and your father may have added to that at our magic pool. So all in all there may have been sixty or seventy pounds of gold. How much is in this bag, Finn?'

Finn hefted the bag again.

'I'd say maybe thirty pounds…so you think there might be more?'

Chief Ruma patted Finn on the back and walked back to the stump and talked to Selum.

Selum turned and went back into the dark cavity. In moments he was back in the entrance again. He held up another bag, and everyone shouted, including Finn.

Finn took this second heavy bag from Selum, untied the thong, and dumped the bag's contents on the ground next to the other nuggets.

'Is that it, Selum?'

Selum nodded, laughing, not understanding Finn's English.

He called to Chief Ruma and spoke in words too rapid for Finn to totally understand, pointing to the horse and to Oakum who stood with his hands on his hips smiling.

Ruma gave commands, and the Indians gathered at one side of the stump which lay on its side and began to push, but the stump was too massive for them to move it. Oakum brought the horse to the other side and looped a rope around one of the stump limbs emanating from the main trunk near the top. Then they tried again, and the stump began to tilt. Finally with one huge push, the stump turned upside down with the trunk vertical, and landed with a thump on the ground. To Finn it felt like a small earthquake.

Now Ruma gave more commands, and the stump was tilted back and forth several times. Then the group pulled the stump over so that it landed on its side again.

In the space where the stump had been turned upside down, lay eight bags just like the other two.

Finn rushed to the spot and began to heft the bags, one by one.

'Ruma, my Dad had more gold than I thought.' He studied the ten bags for a few moments.

'This is just a quick guess, but I'd say each of these bags weighs about thirty pounds. That's 480 ounces x $20.67 per ounce is almost $10,000 per bag. And there's ten bags.

'We're looking at almost $100,000 in gold!'

Finn grabbed Oakum and danced around in circles. The big Indian laughed and laughed, happy to see Finn so excited.

Finn stopped dancing and turned toward the small group of Maidu Indians.

'Whatever the weight, my friends, you have just saved the Kerry Orchards and my family. How can I ever repay you? Here,' he said picking up one of the bags. 'Take this gold. You've earned it. Let me add this to your account at the Chico bank.'

Finn surveyed the beaming faces. Most of the boys had never dealt with a bank before, so they were not sure what Finn was suggesting.

Chief Ruma pushed the proffered bag aside and put his hand on Finn's shoulder.

'Fruit Chief, you have taught my people to grow their own food. For that you have saved the lives of our tribe. That is reward enough. We are happy that we have found your father's gold.'

Finn hugged the Chief and for once, neither of them knew what else to say. Chief Ruma and the boys helped Finn carry the gold to the porch, and then the Indians gathered their tools, mounted their horses and rode off toward the Maidu village. The pile of stumps in the field was still burning fiercely. Finn watched the fire for some time, and finally turned to the pile of ten bags, emptied the bags onto an old quilt lying on the porch swing and left it lying on the edge of the porch, eager to show it to Hannah and his mother when they returned. He looked down at his clothes and realized that he still wore his deputy outfit and badge, and hadn't removed his gun belt yet.

Twenty minutes later, Finn still sat on the front porch almost in tears, waiting for his family to get home, the gold spread out on the quilt before him. Big was stretched out on the step below Finn watching him as Finn unconsciously stroked the big Lab.

Finn couldn't wait to tell his family the great news. He had taken the fruit scale from the shed and had weighed all of the gold. He had been correct about the weight of a bag. The actual weight was over 31 pounds each, which made the total value of the gold over $100,000.

The Kerry's were rich!

He heard a horse's hoofs and, thinking it was his family returning, dashed down the porch steps and stopped as he saw Brett Trask ride into his front yard.

Trask rode over intending to find out whether Finn had cleared the stumps or not.

Big charged out into the yard, circled Trask's horse, and barked protectively.

'Get that damned dog away from my horse, Kerry. He's making Velvet nervous,' he said, fingering his pistol.

Finn gave Trask a nasty look and called Big.

'Big come.' Big went to Finn and sat down next to him, emitting a deep intermittent growl low in his throat.

Trask dismounted, looked at the gold on the porch, and his hopes sank because he knew what had happened.

'What the...what's this, Finn?'

'Brett, the Indians found my father's gold. It was in a big old oak tree stump. I knew it was here on our property somewhere, but we couldn't find it. My father hid it in a most unlikely place...' Finn thought for a moment as he gazed at Trask. 'If it hadn't been for you, we might never have found the gold, Brett. You saved the Kerry Orchards!'

He clasped Trask with both arms and hugged him. Trask stood stunned by the news, his arms limp at his sides as he glanced greedily over Finn's shoulder at the pile of gold nuggets.

Trask's mind worked fast. This changed his plans, he realized. Finn would not be selling him the Kerry property now, and Trask would not get the gold. Thinking quickly, he asked, 'Where's your family and the Maidu Indians? Are they all gone?'

Finn waved his hands about him, his mind still excited by the pile of gold.

'Yes, the Indians went home, and my family will be here by dark.'

Trask realized that this was his last chance at the gold, and he had to take it.

'So there's no one here but you and me, right? Then you leave me no choice, Finn. I'm sorry it had to come to this. I knew Sean's gold was here somewhere. That's why I wanted your property, so I could find it. But I guess I outsmarted myself, asking you to clear those damned stumps.'

Trask pulled his gun and aimed it at Finn.

'Brett, what are you doing?'

'I want that gold, Finn. Sorry I have to do this,' he said and aimed point-blank at Finn.

Big charged forward, leaped at Trask, and hit his gun hand just as Trask fired.

Finn fell backward against the porch steps, his hand clutching the right side of his chest as his shooter's reflexes and the need for self-preservation forced his pistol out of the holster, cocked the hammer, raised his arm and fired once, hitting Trask in the middle of his forehead.

Caught by surprise, Trask was beginning to cock the hammer on his pistol again when he felt the sharp pain, and realized that Finn had shot him. He staggered across the yard, with Big tearing at his pants leg, grabbed at his saddle horn, but fell like a sack of stones, dead before he hit the ground. Big stood over Trask with his front paws on his chest.

Finn stared at Trask's body in disbelief, and then he felt the pain in the side of his chest, and looked down. A bloody spot had spread in a circle on the side of his shirt, and Finn sat on the top step and leaned back against the post.

When Hannah and Jennifer returned from town, they found Finn sitting on the porch steps with his back against the wall, blood oozing from his shirt, and Trask dead on the ground by his horse. Big lay below Finn, his head on Finn's feet.

Hannah and his mother stared in amazement at the mound of gold on the quilt, and then coming out of the daze, Jennifer shook Hannah's arm and they took Finn into the house. As Hannah carried Finn across the porch toward the door, her eyes remained fixed on the pile of gold. She turned toward the house and yelled to Ryan.

'Ryan, take your Blue and ride to Chico for Dr. Bryant. Tell him to be quick. Your father's been shot. Hurry, Ryan.'

Ryan dashed for the stable, and soon Blue trotted out of the stall and Ryan spurred him into a gallop.

Finn was in a daze. He looked at Big sitting by the door.

'Hannah, I think Big saved my life. Trask was…'

Jennifer pushed his head down. 'Be quiet, Finn. Let me look at this wound…'

'Hannah, did you see it? Daddy's gold…on the front porch. It was hidden in a tree stump all these years, and Trask came and…he wanted our gold.'

'Hush up, Finn,' said Jennifer as she cut his shirt away from his side. 'Just lie quiet while Hannah and I tend to this wound. Hmm, looks like it may have gone wide of your vitals. It went out the back, too; maybe hit a rib on the way through, so we need to work on stopping this bleeding. And we'll bandage your chest till the doc gets here.'

When Dr. Bryant finally arrived, he and Jennifer cleaned Finn's wound, applied what antiseptic was necessary, and applied thick bandages around his chest.

'You did a fine job with this wound, Jennifer. You ever consider a job as a nurse? I could sure use one.'

'Hmm. Used to be one in Wadsworth, Nevada, Doc, but never thought about applying here. I'm just a home-maker since I married Sean Kerry. Now that you mention it, I *do* have time on my hands sometimes. What would a nurse make, I mean, roughly?'

Doctor Bryant laughed.

'Why don't you ride into Chico tomorrow afternoon and we can have dinner and talk about it?'

While Jennifer was busy with the doctor and Finn, Hannah, now curious, turned toward the front door, walked slowly out to the porch and stared in awe at the pile of gold. Her hand went to her mouth, and tears rolled down her cheeks. She picked up a handful of nuggets and looked at them without really focusing.

'Thank you, Sean,' she whispered. 'Thank you for saving our family.'

She brought the children out on the porch.

'Ryan, come and see your father's gold.'

* * *

In the weeks that followed, while Finn lay in the hospital recuperating, he made a list of tools he needed replaced because of thefts. On Hannah's next trip to Chico, Bill Mackey guarded the Kerry gold in the wagon, carried the ten bags into the bank, and in a half hour the gold was weighed and deposited in Stillman's safe. Stillman stared at the gold in amazement. Hannah was not in any shape to handle the heavy gold bags, since her pregnancy was well along now, and Dr. Bryant suspected she might have twins this time.

Hannah walked out of the bank with a deposit slip and a stack of bank notes, and kept glancing at the notes as she walked back to the wagon with Bill. Then she stopped, turned and looked across the street at the general store, and turned to Bill.

'Bill, I'm going to Simm's store for a few minutes for Finn. Why don't you go have a drink on the Kerrys? Just tell the bartender to put it on our tab. Wait; does Finn *have* a tab at the saloon, Bill?'

'If he don't, he will have by the time I leave. See you back at the wagon. Need me to bring it over to the store, Hannah?'

She nodded and walked across the street, up the steps, and down the walk to Simm's store, walked in, and gave the list to Jon Simms.

'Like to get all the tools on my list as soon as possible, Jon.'

He toted up the cost and looked at her with a downcast expression.

'Hannah, those tools will cost $450 at least. Can you afford that?'

Hannah smiled and produced her pile of bank notes.

'I'm sure this will cover it, Mr. Simms. We found Sean's gold, and we just finished putting it in the bank this morning. Bill Mackey is bringing the wagon for me.'

Simms face brightened. He walked quickly to the window and saw Bill Mackey coming out of the saloon with several men following him, listening to his story about the gold. Simms took the stack of bank notes and counted them.

'This will more than cover the tools, Mrs. Kerry.'

She grinned and put a finger to her chin. 'Mr. Simms, Don't we owe you some money for your credit to us these last few months?'

He looked sheepish for a moment.

'Well, yes,' he said as he opened a ledger under the counter. He flipped several pages, ran his finger down a column of names, looked at the amount, and laughed.

''Cording to this, you owe me $343, Mrs. Kerry, but wait just a dad-burn minute here. All the days when the Gold Rush was ridin' high, I was makin' big profits off of Finn's fruits, so why don't we just call our bill square?'

'I'll tell Finn that our bill has been cancelled, Mr. Simms. Thank you.'

'I'm mighty happy for you'all, Mrs. Kerry. 'Bout time you had some good breaks.'

He thought for a moment.

'You know, Mrs. Kerry, I was about to ask Finn to set up a new fruit contract with me now that the economy has stabilized. I'll be lookin' forward to seein' your healthy fruits in my store again.'

'Mrs. Kerry? You might tell Finn I have some new irrigation pipe, case he's interested.'

'I'll be sure to tell Finn, Mr. Simms. Thank you. Good day.'

Hannah had been busy now that the economic climate in California had returned to normal. She approached all of their old customers in Chico and beyond, and found many of them interested in renewing their contracts on a smaller scale with Kerry Orchards. Not hard to understand, thought Hannah, since theirs was the only orchard still in operation in this part of the country. Several others had gone bust during the slide in the gold rush.

One night Hannah, with a big smile, showed Jennifer their business ledger.

'Look, mom, we're actually beginning to put money away again. Kerry Orchards is recovering just fine.'

Jennifer hugged her.

'Oh, Hannah, I'm so glad. I know Finn will be pleased. You two have done a wonderful job of keeping the business running during all this gold rush mess.'

Jennifer smiled.

'I have some news, too, Hannah. I've taken a job with Dr. Bryant in

Chico. He wants me to be his nurse. He's taking me to dinner tonight so we can discuss my duties. He's such a nice man. Handsome, too. Reminds me a little of Sean...'

Hannah looked at Jennifer and smiled knowingly.

'Good luck, mom.'

At Finn's request, Bill Mackey spent some time at the Kerry home in the next three weeks, directing the extension of the barn with stalls for Martin and Blue. Mackey had the fifteen unused acres well-fenced so that Martin could roam free and graze to his heart's content in his old age. Bill smiled when he looked over the distant fence toward the Trask place. He could see Mrs. Trask directing Mort Persons as he packed her possessions onto his large wagon for her move.

Fine piece of property that Trask land, he mused to himself. Wonder if Finn has any inclinations on expanding. Maybe I'll ask Mr. Stillman if he knows the price. A man could do worse than have a piece of land like that. And with those growing youngsters, in a few years, Finn might just want to expand his orchards.

* * *

While Finn was in the hospital in Chico, the Maidu Indian boys under the direction of Chief Ruma and his new wife, Aida, tended the orchards, and began the apricot harvest.

Before his release from the hospital, the Sheriff visited Finn and asked him to tell what had happened the day he shot Trask.

'Pretty straightforward, Sheriff. Trask wanted my father's gold. Somehow he found out about it; I think through some loose talk from the Indian boys. When he came to our place and saw all that gold lying on the porch, he got desperate, and shot me and I shot him back. Guess my shot was more effective.'

'Okay, Finn. Obviously a case of self defense. Let's leave it at that. You get well now, hear?'

By September, Finn was released from the hospital and Hannah, his mother, Ryan, and Megan came to take him home in the wagon. Ryan hugged his father long and hard, and Megan crawled into the rear of the wagon with Finn and snuggled into his arms under his blanket for the trip home.

'Would you stop by Mort Persons Livery Stable for a minute?' asked Finn.

They pulled up, and Mort walked out and shook Finn's hand warmly.

'Good to see you up and around again, Finn.'

Finn looked at him with a question on face.

'Did you get it, Mort?' He asked in a near-whisper.

Mort nodded and smiled.

'Guess you know that Mrs. Trask is moving back to Kentucky to live with her folks. Poor woman.'

Mort winked at Finn as they pulled away with Hannah driving. When they arrived home, Finn got out of the wagon with Hannah's help.

'Hannah, would you help me into the parlor?'

She took his elbow and led him into the parlor and stopped. Hannah looked in the corner and put her hands over her mouth. Her old Bosendorfer piano sat by the window with a sparkling shine, a new matching piano bench, and a big bouquet of red roses on the piano cover. She turned to Finn and threw her arms around him.

'Oh, Finn…'

Ryan called Big, and he and Big walked in with Ryan's hand on the back of the Lab; the Lab looked as big as Ryan. Finn laughed as the huge yellow dog bounded across the floor, put his feet on Finn and licked Finn's cheek.

'For the runt of the litter, he sure is Big,' Finn said as he stroked the huge lab's head.

* * *

As Finn sat on the porch with a quilt over him, he started to rise, but his mother pushed him back down gently. 'You just rest there, Finn. The more rest you get the quicker you'll be on your feet and out in that orchard again. The Indian boys have missed you.'

From the porch, Finn looked over their orchards and hugged his mother, Hannah, and the children.

'Looking out on our orchards, I remember what dad said to me the night he died.

197

'He said, 'Finn, nothing I'd like better than to walk outside and see the blue of the mountains in the early morning, feel that warm California breeze and the sun on my skin, see our fruit growing, and watch the clouds go by. Finn, there's gold in those orchards, so everything will be all right...'

'I guess I didn't understand what dad meant at that time, about gold in the orchards, but I do now. He loved these orchards and so do I. *They* are our gold.

'I want to do the same thing–every morning of my life. And now we have the means to fix the place up right and live decent again, thanks to Dad...'

He looked up as he heard Hannah playing her new piano, the one he had repurchased from Cecelia Trask before she left for Kentucky where her family lived.

'Now there's a sound I've missed lately. Say, mom, I'll bet Hannah and I could be a duo with her on the piano and me on the flute.'

His mother grinned.

'Yes, you two do make a fine duo.'

Hannah stopped playing and joined them on the porch. She bent and kissed Finn on the forehead.

'The new sheriff visited me in the hospital, Hannah. He asked me if I still wanted to be his deputy. I told him no. My gun-toting days are over.

'From now on the Kerry family will be full-time orchardists–

'rich orchardists.'

Epilogue

In 1870, Finn Kerry reviewed the Maidu Indian situation.

In 1848 in California, Indians composed 92,000 to 150,000 of the population. By 1855, the Indian population had decreased to about 30,000 due to killings, diseases, massacres, and movement of tribes out of California.

Alternately, the influx of gold prospectors from Europe and Asia swelled California to over 300,000 by 1855. They were called the '49-ers'. Some said it was as high as 500,000.

Many Indians were forcibly removed from their traditional tribal lands by miners, ranchers, and farmers, and even by the California government. The Indian's situation became so bad that the people in many villages were massacred by whites in order to free their lands.

The first governor of California, Peter Burnett, called for 'complete extermination of all Indian tribes in California' (genocide). 'Removal' was the dominant policy in California, one way or another.

From the gold rush days to the 1870's the California tribes were declared 'extinct'. None (even the Yamadi Maidu) had preserved their cultural way of life as hunters. Even the Yamadi Maidu had changed from a hunter society to an agricultural society, but by desire, not by command.

By the 1850's Indians were put in many small reservations and rancheros. California had become a state on September 9, 1850. The Indians received no help from the California government, and the lands they were moved to, had no natural resources which made them unsuitable for farming–which was the thing the government suggested they be taught.

Finn Kerry was a great help in overcoming some of these obstacles.

He helped the Maidu develop fertilizers to bring the poor earth to life, by buying them small herds of horses to be used in their fertilizer composts, in plowing, and for transportation. He procured seeds and the farm implements necessary for the Maidu to strengthen their new agriculture. And he did this with the Maidu's own gold.

By the clever use of words in laws pertaining to Indians, they became 'enslaved' in the 1850's and 60's. They had no status as citizens, and therefore no civil rights. No one listened to the Maidu Indians, so they had to 'disappear' from the white man's sight in order to exist.

Several Federal agents (Redick McKee, George W. Barbour, and O.M. Wozencraft) were given the job of making treaties with the Indians. These treaties set aside 18 reserves for the Indians.

With these treaties came promises from the Federal government of aid in the form of schools, farming instruction, farm equipment, seed, cloth, and housing. Little of this aid was ever forthcoming. By the 1870's, according to government sources, the Indians 'had disappeared from view'.

A treaty with the Nisenan Maidu was declared null and void by the government due to lobbies by large business interests.

The U.S. Government did not recognize the rights of Indians to lease, sell, or rent their lands.

Slavery was abolished for African Americans, but not for the Indians. The Indians faced 'indentured servitude', so men, women, and children were forced into slavery unless they had a thriving culture–and did not encroach on lands desired by white men.

In truth, the Indians were sent to the most desolate areas and the most useless lands.

Although the white man's domination of the plains tribes was still in the future, through Finn's efforts, at last the Yamadi Maidu gold had become something of value in their new reservation home. Their new culture was held up as a model for other Indian tribes, but few Indians besides the Maidu were interested in farming, and so other tribes sank into sloth and drunkenness, and blamed the white man.

The Yamadi Maidu were one of the few California tribes to take hold of their own destiny partly due to the help of Finn Kerry.

Appendix

Some readers might be interested in gold conversions, and how much Sean Kerry's gold was worth.

Gold

Price of one ounce of gold in 1848 = $20.67/oz. (Stayed the same up to 1933)

Weight of gold: = 0.698 lb. / cu.in.

Gold gathered by Indians

Maidu Boy's gold	= 2 lb each	
Total 8 boys		= 16 lb.
Maidu Boy's gold	= 3 lb. each	
Total 8 boys		= 24 lb.

Total weight of gold from boys = 40 lb.

Gold gathered by Sean

Sean accumulated lbs. per trip	= 45 lb.	
Sean made 6 trips to pool: total lbs.		= 270 lb.

Total weight from boys and Sean = 310 lb.

Approximate size of Sean's gold

Volume of 1 bag to carry Sean's gold = 5h x 2.98w x 2.98d = 44.4 cu.in.

Weight per bag = 44.4 x 0.698 (lb/cu.in) = 31.0 lb.

Weight of 10 bags of nuggets = 310 lb.

Gold total worth   (@ $20.67/ounce) = $102,523

Story Bibliography

Agriculture
http://www.almanac.com/plant/pears
http://www.ces.ncsu.edu/depts/hort/hil/ag29.html
http://ucanr.edu/sites/sacmg/Fruit_and_nuts/

Maidu Indians
http://www.maidu.com/maiduculture/culture.html#
 marriage
http://www.mechoopda-nsn.gov/history/life.asp
http?://www.maidu.com/maiduculture/culture.html#
 trade

Weapons
http://en.wikipedia.org/wiki/Colt_Pocket_Percussio
 n_Revolvers
http://www.bing.com/videos/search?
 q=youtube.colt+baby+dragoon+pistol&FORM=
 VIRE11#view=detail&mid=86A5B4DFD73570
 DD0D6886A5B4DFD73570DD0D68

California Gold Rush
http://www.kidport.com/reflib/usahistory/calgoldrus
 h/lifeof49ers.htm

California/Nevada Area
En.wikipedia.org/wiki/feather_river
http://www.bing.com/images/search?
 q=Map+of+Lower+Sacramento+River&Form=IQFRDR#
 view=detail&id=74BEC446A6A8E258E03E1FCEF0082
 59B2B64CD38&selectedIndex=0